THE HAUNTING OF DRANG ISLAND

Arthur G. Slade

ORCA BOOK PUBLISHERS

Copyright © 1998 Arthur G. Slade

Canadian Cataloguing in Publication Data
Slade, Arthur G. (Arthur Gregory)
  The haunting of Drang Island

  ISBN 1-55143-111-4

  I. Title.
PS8587.L343H38 1998   jc813'.54   C98-910783-3
PZ7.S628835Ha 1998

Library of Congress Catalog Card Number: 98-85663

Orca Book Publishers gratefully acknowledges the support of our publishing
programs provided by the following agencies: the Department of Canadian
Heritage, The Canada Council for the Arts, and the British Columbia Arts
Council.

Cover design by Christine Toller
Cover painting and interior illustrations by Ljuba Levstek
Printed and bound in Canada

Orca Book Publishers   Orca Book Publishers
PO Box 5626, Station B   PO Box 468
Victoria, BC Canada   Custer, WA   USA
V8R 6S4   98240-0468

98 99 00   5 4 3 2 1

This one's for Brenda, with love.

And to all those unheralded English teachers out there.

This book also has a redhead in it, so I want to thank Lucy Maud Montgomery for inventing that spirited Canadian redhead from Green Gables. Oddly enough, L.M.M. was the third cousin of my great grandmother Anna Jean Frost of P.E.I., so I can actually lay claim to some of the same genes.

I also want to thank Brenda Baker, Barbara Sapergia and Anne Slade, three women who helped in the shaping of this book. And my Grandma Jean for always being such a great support.

And finally, thanks to Bob Tyrrell for some timely suggestions that opened up a whole new world of possibilities on Drang.

If you're looking for Drang Island, it's a ways past the north end of Vancouver Island. Keep your eyes peeled for thick fog, mist, tall cliff walls and lightning. It can sometimes be very hard to find. Don't believe anyone who tells you it doesn't exist.

» 1 «

If you're gonna die, die with your boots on.

That's what my Grandpa Thursten used to say. It was the Viking code. "Remember, Michael," he'd whisper in his harsh, gravelly voice, "face whatever life has to throw at you with gritted teeth and grim determination. Never surrender."

I wished he'd given me a few more details. Like what to do if you and your father were stuffed into life jackets and trapped on the wild ocean in a tiny ferry piloted by a man who was three times as old as God. And let's say all the forces of nature were trying their best to send you to the bottom of that ocean, while lightning tore holes in the sky. Wind ripped the breath from your lungs. Waves pummeled you. *What would you suggest we do then, Gramps?*

I gripped the side of the boat. Dad was right next to me, one hand clamped on the bench.

A little more than thirty hours ago I was tapping my pen against my desk, waiting for the school bell to ring and finally announce the end of grade nine and the start of summer. At the time I was looking forward to getting away from a year of bad marks and failed friendships. If someone said I could beam myself back to that same desk right now and live my last year over again, I'd almost do it. Almost.

Harbard, the ferryman, faced Dad and me. "One of you will not return," he announced.

"What?" Dad yelled, struggling to be heard above the noise of the engine and the crashing waves. He had his baseball hat on backwards to prevent the gale from ripping it off. His round-rimmed glasses dripped with water. "What did you say?"

Harbard turned his head and glared, his deep-set eyes burning with anger, almost like he was mad that he'd allowed us on his ferry, that the storm was our fault. He looked as if he hadn't slept, shaved, or had a haircut since the sixties. Who would give this guy a license to run a boat?

He stared right at me. Could he read my mind? I leaned even harder against the back of the ferry, squirming away from his gaze.

"One of you will not return. I will take you both to Drang Island tonight, but only one will come back with me. It is *örlög:* fate."

A wave hurled itself against the bow, spraying us with water. Dad shielded his face. "You can stop kidding around, now," he said, half joking.

Harbard was staring forward again, fighting to keep the boat steady. He shook his head, making his yellow seaman's cap move back and forth. "No jest, not tonight. The Norns decree the shape of our lives, regardless of our wishes."

"You're scaring the heck out of me and Michael," Dad shouted into the gale. He sounded serious. I don't think Harbard heard him this time, at least he didn't make any reply to show he had.

"I'm not frightened," I said, quietly, "really, I'm not."

Dad glanced down at me. People always commented on how similar we were; we both had blue eyes and the same long, thin-boned features passed down to us by our Icelandic ancestors. The only difference was my father had sandy-blonde hair and mine was almost black. But I hoped I wasn't looking at all like Dad right now. There was an expression on his face I'd never seen before. Not fear, but something close to fear. He clenched his teeth; his jaw muscles bulged. He seemed like he was about to speak, then he turned away and stared across the ocean.

I followed Dad's gaze. By squinting my eyes I could pick out glowing spheres in the distance, zigzagging all around like restless fireflies and occasionally blinking out. They were the lights of the park, our destination. At least there was electricity on the island. We already had a spot reserved in the campground. But would we ever get there? I was sure we'd been lurching through the water for more than an hour since leaving Port Hardy. And every second seemed to be bringing us closer to the ends of the earth.

Another huge wave struck like a battering ram, forcing the boat to lean. It knocked Dad and me to the edge of the bench. The ferry kept tipping in the same direction. It felt like a huge hand was pushing one side upwards. The motor sputtered and several moments passed where I couldn't hear anything. Just silence. The boat leaned farther, so far that water began lapping over the side.

And I had the sudden feeling this was more than a wave; something bigger, underneath, lifting us higher.

And higher.

Then, just when I thought we were about to be tossed overboard, a clap of thunder crackled through the sky. The boat fell back the other way, crashed down into the water and leveled out again. Harbard gunned the engine.

"Jormungand just turned over," Harbard said. The first word sounded like *yourmungond*. He rubbed at something hanging on his neck. A good-luck charm? "The god of the deeps spared us. This time. Many a ship has gone down in this very spot. Last year twelve sailors drowned. They found part of the hull. Nothing more."

"What's he talking about?" I whispered to Dad, trying my best to be tactful. "Is he nuts?"

My father put his finger to his lips, motioning me to be silent. "They told me back at port that this can be a bad stretch of water. But there was no sign of a storm when we left." He paused, glanced at Harbard. "And despite his looks, our ferryman came highly recommended. He's even part Icelandic."

Well, I should have seen that from the beginning. The crazy eyes, the need to talk about doom and gloom. Being Icelandic myself, I knew we were a race of people stuffed full of long stories and weird ideas. And it got worse as we got older. My Grandpa Thursten is the perfect example of that. He's eighty or so and all he talks about now is people coming back from the dead, or trolls chewing on the bones of sheep, or Norsemen yelling insults at each other from their boats.

Don't get me wrong. Grandpa's a fun guy. You just have to get used to his dark sense of humor.

Of course, after everything that happened while I was staying with him last summer, I took anything any Icelandic person said a lot more seriously. "Which … which one's Jormungand, Dad? Is he the giant wolf the Viking gods have to bind?"

Dad shook his head. "I don't want to get into all that stuff now."

"Well … just give me the short version."

Dad smiled. Maybe he wasn't as nervous as I thought. "Jormungand is the big snake who lives under the ocean and wraps himself around the whole world. He spends his time biting his own tail and swallowing whales that are unlucky enough to pass near him."

"Is he friendly?"

"No. Loki, the most evil and trickiest of the gods, and the giantess Angrboda had three monstrous children, each with enough power to destroy the gods. Jormungand was one of them. He started out as just a little snake, but Odin knew how dangerous this monster would become. He threw him in the ocean and Jormungand grew gigantic. He waits down there until the end of the world—Ragnarok. The final, vicious battle between the gods and the giants. Jormungand is killed by Thor, the god with the hammer. Then Thor stumbles back nine steps and falls down dead, poisoned by Jormungand's venom."

"Oh. I see." Well, that was enough about that. Why weren't there any happy Norse stories? Ones where the good guys win in the end and everyone lives to a ripe old age. Or how about one where three travelers on a ferry don't sink in the ocean and become fish food?

Dad was staring into the distance again, lost in thought. We carried on without speaking, the boat's engine alternating between roaring and gasping as it struggled through the watery turmoil. The lights gradually came closer, turning into a sparse set of streetlamps set far inside a cove. A few small buildings were visible, huddled close together.

They looked tiny compared to what surrounded them— tall spires and walls of jagged rock standing high in the air. We passed so close to a finger of stone that I could have reached out and run my hand along its chipped surface. How many boats had it claimed? For a split second a bolt of lightning illuminated the cliffs. Every corner seemed sharp and unassailable, every crag dangerous.

So this was Drang Island. Who would want to call this place home? It looked about as friendly as Harbard's face.

We came out of the open water and into the bay. The waves were calmer here and for the first time I relaxed my grip on the side of the ferry. I got a good look at the buildings on the beach. They were cabins, old and unkempt, facing the water. Only one had light coming from the window. Behind them was a thick collection of trees, their branches reaching down toward the rooftops. A path had been cut through the trees, lit by two dim streetlamps. I assumed that would be the way to the campground.

We pulled up to a deserted wooden wharf and Harbard tossed a rope around a post and secured the boat. Dad and I gathered our gear and bikes and stepped onto solid wood. My legs felt all wobbly. My balance was off center. It was as if some part of me was still on the water, rocking back and forth. I planted my feet firmly and sucked in some air, then let out a long sigh. It was hard to believe that most of my ancestors had spent their lives on the wide open ocean. Tonight, I just wanted to be a landlubber.

We handed back our life jackets, then Dad started digging in his wallet for our fare. When we'd first boarded the ferry, Harbard had explained that he only accepted payment for his services after he reached the other side, just in case something happened on the way there. He'd said this with a slight smile at the time.

But now there was no smile. Harbard shook his head and motioned for Dad to put his money away. He stared silently, his gaze going back and forth between us. I had no idea what he was searching for. Behind all that hair and sunken face, he looked sad. A small version of Thor's hammer hung from a metal chain around his neck—it *was* a good-luck charm. "Your futures are not entirely clear," he whispered, hoarsely, "but I know one thing; it would be ill luck to take money from the doomed." Then he undid the mooring and limped to the front of the boat. Did he have a peg leg? I wondered. Harbard backed the ferry out of the dock, gunned the motor and steered toward the open water, leaving us staring at his retreating figure.

I looked at Dad. "What did all that mean?"

"I have no idea." He patted my shoulder. "It's probably nothing. We all get a little stranger as we get older." He scrunched up his shoulders, did his best Hunchback of Notre Dame impression. "See, it's happening to me already." I laughed and clapped politely.

Dad bowed, then lifted his backpack and used his right hand to guide his bike. "Pick up your stuff and don't forget anything, okay?"

"I won't." You'd think I had Alzheimer's the way Dad was talking. I grabbed my own backpack and bike.

Dad pulled up the collar on his coat and motioned me ahead with a nod. "I'd guess we're not too far from the campground. On the way we can stop at the Park Office, call home, and tell your mom and your sister we made it safe and sound. Your mom will be up late waiting for the call, I bet. But we better hurry. It feels like it might rain."

It did rain.

Hard. The forty days and forty nights kind that threatens to wash away everything on earth.

Luckily we'd found our little camping spot and had just finished putting up our three-person tent when the first drop made its splashy appearance right on the top of my head. We ducked inside. Dad flicked on the battery-powered plastic lamp and we unrolled our sleeping bags, unpacked the rest of our gear and rewarded ourselves with a granola bar snack.

The tent felt safe, which calmed me down, because our walk through the campground had been unnerving. The place was as empty and about as welcoming as a ghost town, site after empty site lit by the occasional outdoor lamp set high on a post. The one good thing was the Park Office, a deserted log cabin where the phone actually worked and we were able to call home. When we were done, I pointed at a big sign on the wall that read WARNING: THE GENERATOR SHUTS DOWN AT 11:00 PM. Realizing we only had a few minutes, Dad and I ran to our site. We made it about halfway there before the lights blinked out, so we had to set up the tent with the help of a flashlight.

Safely inside, I listened to the rain. A million watery drummers drummed on the sides of our new home; it was beginning to feel like we might be in for two weeks of this. Even still, chances were good that I'd have more fun here than back in Missouri. On Drang I wouldn't have to try and make a whole new set of friends, like I'd had to last winter. Tried and failed, that is. I'd just started high school and unfortunately my two closest pals, the only people I really knew well in Chillicothe, had moved halfway through the school year and I wasn't able to find anyone else to hang around with. My twin sister, Sarah, had managed to fit in just like that. But she always seemed to be better than me at most things that involved making friends. And using her head.

For instance, she probably wouldn't have taken Dad's car out for a test-drive in the middle of winter. Especially not a year and a half before getting her license.

Anyway, that's something I'd rather forget.

There was another good thing about our trip; I was getting to spend time with Dad. You see, between looking after the farm, training bird dogs and doing his writing, Dad's a busy guy. To be entirely honest, I was surprised when he asked me to come to Drang. If he was only going to choose one of his children, I would've placed all bets on my sister. They just seemed to get along better.

I crawled into my sleeping bag. Dad had already wrapped himself up in his own downy cocoon, looking like a human caterpillar with glasses. He was jotting notes in his journal. Nearly every night for the last three years he'd been working on a book filled with modern-day Viking tales. It was called *How Odin Lost His Eye* or something equally appetizing. He was extremely secretive about the book; he hadn't let me, Mom or Sarah read a word of it. He said he wanted it to be a surprise when it was published. Part of the reason we'd come here was for him to do research.

"Do you know why they call this place Drang?" Dad asked.

"I haven't got a clue," I answered.

"Some Icelanders made a settlement at the north end. No one's sure when, but probably in the late 1800s. They hoped it would be a safe haven. Close to the salmon. But the island was so inhospitable their village failed and only one hardy soul stayed on. The place reminded them of the original Drang Island, off the north coast of Iceland. You know, where Grettir died."

This was starting to ring a dim bell. "You mean Grettir Asmundson? Our ancestor?"

Dad rolled his eyes. "Your grandfather's been filling you full of tales, hasn't he? There's no easy way to prove we're descended from Grettir the Strong, but Drang *was* where he spent the last years of his life. You could only get up on the isle by using ladders. It was the perfect place for him to hide from his enemy, Thorir. But ever since Grettir had fought an undead monster, he couldn't stand facing darkness alone. The draugr had cursed him, saying he would always see his eyes in the night. So Grettir kept other outlaws as company. One of them was lazy and didn't pull up the ladders. Grettir's enemies braved a storm, made it to the island and climbed up. Grettir was sick and they were able to kill him, but he still wouldn't release his sword. They had to cut off his hand. One man even chopped at Grettir's head and ended up chipping his blade."

"Now I *know* he's related to us. With a head that thick, he has to be."

"Oh, ha, ha." Dad set down his journal. "You know, this island has interested me for years. All sorts of rumors about it have rippled through the Icelandic communities."

"What kind of rumors?"

"Well, they say ghost ships are sometimes spotted in the mist. Viking longboats with dark sails and figureheads in the form of a long-necked monster. But no one's ever been able to board one. And you heard Harbard talk about the snake Jormungand. He actually believes in all the old myths that we only call stories. He was born and raised on this island—that's what the folks said back at Port Hardy. That means he might be a descendant of the original settlers, so I hope I get a chance to ask him about their beliefs."

"We came all this way to talk to that psycho?"

Dad shook his head. "I didn't have a clue that Harbard existed until a few hours ago. But my guess is he knows more about Drang than anyone else. Even his name suggests that: Harbard means Graybeard in the old tongue. It was one of the names Odin used when he disguised himself." Dad rubbed the top of his head, checking to see if his bald spot had grown in. For the thousandth time today. "The real reason I came is because there are supposedly ruins from the original village somewhere on the north end, along with a series of caves that might have served as shelter for the pioneers. I want to see these places. And talk to any locals I can find. Some swear that the fetches of a great Norse sorcerer still flit around the island."

Dad got a kick out of saying strange words and leaving me to guess what they meant. "Fetches?" I asked impatiently.

"*Fylgja* they were called in Old Icelandic. Dark spirits created by a mage well-versed in the unearthly arts. He'd take his soul and make mirror images of it, then send them out to do his bidding. These fetches were used to spy on the enemy, to cause a disturbance or to bring bad luck.

They were invisible, unless you had second sight. Sometimes they could even be sent into people's dreams to deliver a message. They apparently helped drive the Icelandic settlers away from Drang."

"I see. This *is* going to be a fun vacation."

"I suppose now would be a bad time to tell you the snake population on Drang is extremely high; for some reason they breed quite rapidly out here, even though it's such a cold climate. There have been a number of studies done, but the scientists can't explain why there are so many snakes."

"Oh, great." I slammed my head into my pillow in fake anger.

"I thought you weren't frightened of snakes."

"I'm not. But there's a difference between not being frightened of snakes and wanting to go to an island full of them."

"Would it help if I told you only three people in Canada have died from snake bites since 1956?"

"My luck, I'd be the fourth."

"Actually, the fourth one might have been a well-known scientist called Doc Siroiska. He came here last year and disappeared on the north part of the island. He was an expert on snakes. Some figure one finally got him."

I shivered. "That's great, Dad! Is this just some clever way to get rid of me?"

"Well, I always did like your sister better," he said lightly. I knew he intended this as a joke, but it still made me do a slow burn. I couldn't help but think it was partly true. Dad fluffed up his pillow, then set it behind his head and laughed. "You look a little scared, Michael. Cheer up! Tomorrow's going to be a grand day." He took off his glasses and placed them carefully in their case. "Goodnight."

I just nodded. Dad clicked off the light. About three seconds later he began to snore lightly. Was this a side effect of growing old?

I lay there, staring up into the darkness. I didn't feel quite ready to sleep.

A *schlick* sound came from outside the tent. Followed by a harsh, almost growling noise.

Bears? I strained my brain, trying to recall if Dad had at any time mentioned creatures larger than snakes. I couldn't come up with a thing. It was probably just a stray dog.

The rain stopped. Dad's snoring didn't.

A can rattled.

I sat up. Dad was dead to the world. I thought briefly of waking him, then decided against it. I could check this out on my own. Grandpa had always said, "Fearlessness is better than a faint heart for any man who pokes his nose out of doors."

I found my jeans, threw on shoes and a shirt, grabbed the flashlight and poked my nose out of doors.

A short distance away a branch snapped.

» 3 «

It took awhile for my eyes to adjust. I crouched next to the tent, head cocked to one side, listening. A pale moon sent a few slivers of silver light through the pine trees, illuminating the abundance of plants and tall grass at the edge of the campground. Tendrils of mist floated a couple of inches above the ground. The air was muggy and smelled of damp, rotting vegetation.

A dull, repetitive, thudding noise started, then stopped. I swallowed and took a few steps toward the echoes, clutching the flashlight tightly. I didn't turn it on for fear of attracting attention to myself. The small road at the edge of our campsite was clear and straight. I could follow it and still be within sight of our tent.

I crept up to the road. Now metal was ringing against metal. I carried on, step by step, my shoes sinking in mud. Water soaked through the sides and into my socks. Before I knew it, I had turned a corner and couldn't see our campsite anymore. The sounds grew louder.

Rain still dripped down from the trees. I padded ahead, careful to avoid any large puddles, moving as silently as I could.

A dark shape flitted across the track about five feet from

me, eyes glowing with pale yellow light. I jumped back. Leaves rattled as the creature disappeared into the brush.

Cat, I thought. It had to be a big black cat. It was the same shape. And just as fast.

I forced myself to go forward. This was stupid. If my sister were here, she'd have told me exactly the same thing. Or said something wise like, "Fearlessness is better than a faint heart, unless it's dark and you're alone."

I was too curious to go back now. Not before I caught a glimpse of who—or what—was making the noise. I rounded another bend.

A strange gray form shifted in the wind, going up and down. At first it looked like the back of a giant, ghostly bear, shaking itself. It grew larger, filled with air, then deflated and fell. I couldn't make sense of what I was seeing.

Someone cursed.

I took another hesitant step and things began to come together. It was a tent. A camper was trying to set it up in the middle of the night. So we *weren't* the only residents of the park.

I squinted. A black figure was bent over, hammering another spike into the ground and grunting, but it was a tricky job without any light.

I cleared my throat.

The banging continued.

I cleared it again. Louder.

The person stood straight up, held the tool like a weapon. "Who's there?" a gruff, muffled voice asked. "This is an axe. I'm not afraid to use it! Who's there?"

"Uh … I am."

The camper wore a waterproof sports jacket and stood a few inches shorter than me. The hood was up, hiding any features. The hatchet glinted in the moonlight. Small and sharp. "Be more specific! Do you have a name?"

"Yeah, it's Michael. Do you need some help?"

"No. Bug off!"

I took a step back. "Gee. Okay. Just askin'. But I do have a flashlight, you know."

"A flashlight? Why aren't you using it?" the man growled.

"I … uh …"

"Look. Turn it on. Shine it at yourself so I can see who I'm talking to."

So I did. The light blinded me, lit my face from below so I'm sure I looked ghoulish. My nostrils were probably glowing orange. "Oh," the raspy voice said, "you're just a kid."

This ticked me off. "Your turn." I pointed the light at the dark shape, but I couldn't see much. Just a nose and glaring eyes. Then he lowered the hatchet and pulled back his hood, revealing red hair cut short around the ears and two stern, angry eyes.

And soft lips.

My jaw dropped. "You're … a girl!"

"You're quite the detective," she snarled.

"I couldn't tell," I stammered, "it being dark and you talking so raspy." She looked about my age. I stared at her, my eyes wide. She was pretty, with a thin nose and ivory-colored skin dotted with freckles. "Uh … or is that your normal voice?"

"Will you point that light away?" she said, her voice sounding much lighter. She gestured toward the ground. "Better yet, shine it on the tent. That'd be helpful. At least I could pound in these pegs while you stand around in shock."

I lowered the flashlight.

"Thanks," she said. She began wielding the camp axe quickly, hitting the pegs squarely with the blunt end. She'd done this before. "Now point it over there!" she commanded. I moved the beam. She swung again. "And there." I adjusted the angle. A second later another peg was in the ground. She barked a few commands and tightened a rope.

I was still amazed that she was even here. Who was she? What was she doing alone out here in the middle of nowhere?

"Hold this." She gave me a pole. She looped a yellow rope through a hook on the top of the tent, then pulled up on the other side. With a click, her new home was suddenly high in the air and standing firm.

She came around to the front. "Your work is done. You can go now."

"But … but what's your name? How'd you get to the island?"

She laughed. "Don't worry. We seem to be the only people dumb enough to camp here, so I'm sure we'll run into each other again. I'll tell you then. Goodnight."

She slipped into her tent.

I stood there, my mind buzzing. Then, feeling suddenly awkward, like I'd just been dismissed by a teacher, I started for home.

» 4 «

I didn't sleep well. At first I couldn't stop thinking about the girl. Then finally I fell into a fitful slumber. I had a dream that I was at the far end of the island, surrounded by darkness. A thin specter, formed of malice and swirling dark-blue light, rose out of the ground and started walking south, singing softly to himself. I followed, drawn toward him like a magnet. I had the feeling he was searching for something. He made his way over a tree that had fallen across a long, deep crevasse, then he drifted for a distance and finally entered the campground and stole into our tent.

Once there he just glared down at me and Dad, radiating anger and bad luck. I stared up at him, finding it impossible to move. Then the vision suddenly ended and started over. I kept waking up and looking for the visitor, but the shape skulked into the shadows. I'd convince myself I was dreaming, fall asleep again, and end up right back in the same nightmare. Finally, after about half the night had passed, I drifted into sleep. I was exhausted.

Morning brought the sound of Dad humming to himself. I moved my arm and discovered my entire body ached.

"You gonna sleep all day, Michael?" Dad asked. "The early bird gets the worm, you know."

I opened my eyes and shook my head slowly, too tired to groan at Dad's cliché. He was clad in his blue jogging suit, sitting down, tying his shoes.

The sunlight was doing its best to turn the tent into a solarium. Birds chirped in the distance. Drang seemed like a completely different place than it had been eight hours ago.

I attempted to get out of bed, but all the muscles in my back tightened into knots. I forced myself to sit up. It seemed a year had passed since the last time I opened my eyes. Dim, dark shapes flitted in my mind, then vanished.

Dad was bent over, trying to open the tent door. "Some campers we are," he commented, running the zipper to the top. "We didn't even zip the flaps all the way down." He stepped outside.

Then I remembered what had happened last night before I went to sleep. About the girl. I searched around for my cutoffs. Maybe she was awake already. Or did I just imagine her?

Dad huffed and puffed, doing his warm-up exercises to get ready for his daily run. His outline was cast across the tent, a stretched-out cartoon version of him pumping his knees. Then he suddenly stopped. "Oh, my God," he whispered. This was pretty alarming because he never uses the Lord's name in vain. Well, except if the car gets a flat tire.

I did up my shorts and headed outside.

Dad was standing beside the tent, his arms crossed. His face had that slightly red tinge that meant he was getting mad. "I can't believe someone would do this," he said.

There, scrawled across our brand new tent, was some kind of graffiti. The words were bright red and partly blurred by the rain. They said: YU AR MARKED DED.

"It's some kind of tar," Dad said. "It's gonna be near to

impossible to get it off."

I stared at the letters. It looked more like thick blood to me, but I didn't mention that to Dad.

There was a footprint in the mud. It was astounding; so large that whoever made it must have been at least seven feet tall. Alongside it were something like dog's tracks. A gigantic dog.

I felt a chill. It looked like giants had been hanging around our campground.

A gray, partially buried object caught my eye. Three or four feathers lay next to an odd, mud-covered lump. I leaned a little closer.

One of the feathers was stained red. And the lump wasn't a lump at all, but the body of a bird.

A headless pigeon.

Its head rested a few feet away. One dull black eye stared at me. "Dad, take a look," I said.

He came over. "What is—*ohhh*. What kind of vandals would kill a bird?"

"Kids," a voice said from behind us.

» 5 «

We turned. There, blocking out part of the sunlight, stood a heavyset man. He had a bulging stomach, thick arms and wore a uniform with a gray shirt and brown pants. A Park Ranger patch was stitched to his right shoulder. "I'm Dermot Morrison," he said, looking at us over the top of his sunglasses. His voice was deep and he spoke like he was used to having people pay attention to him. "And like I said, it was kids."

"Kids did this?" Dad crossed his arms again.

I wanted to blurt out something about the size of the footprint, but my tongue was tied in a knot.

Ranger Morrison nodded. "Yeah, kids. They hit a few of the tents last night. Out for a fun time. They're bored, spoiled, rich punks who spend the summer here with their parents on the east side of the island. They sneak over to the campground to raise havoc." He smiled and turned away, like he'd just explained everything we needed to know.

"Well, have you caught them yet?" Dad asked.

"No," Ranger Morrison said over his shoulder. "I've got a few things to do before that." He stopped and faced us. "You can't just pick 'em up for nothing. You have to have your case together." He scratched the side of his nose. "But I'll get 'em. Don't worry."

"What's this graffiti supposed to mean?" Dad asked. The last part of his sentence sounded like *s'pose ta mean*.

"You a Yank?" the Ranger asked.

"I'm not sure," Dad answered. Morrison crinkled up his face with a look of utter confusion. "What I mean to say is, we're from Missouri. If you're a Yank, you're from the northern U.S. And Southerners come from the south. Missouri's right on the border between South and North, so I don't know which one I am. Probably a Yank, though."

"I see." The ranger gave us the once-over, as if he was sizing us for jail cells. Or an asylum. "Anyway, the graffiti, as you call it, don't mean nuthin'. They just want to scare people. I wouldn't pay it any attention."

"Should we be worried about them coming back?" Dad asked.

"No. I have a good idea who did this. I'll drop by their cabin today, invite myself in for coffee. That'll scare the crap out of those juvees. Don't you worry, I've got it under control." He eyed us up again, seemed to dare us to contradict him.

"You will tell us when you get them." The way Dad said this, it didn't sound like a question.

Ranger Morrison sniffed. "You'll find out, one way or another." He looked down, seemed to smile. "You should probably put that bird in the garbage. It's gonna be a steamer of a day today and it doesn't take too long for them to start to stinking." He paused, pushed up his sunglasses and nodded to us. "Enjoy your stay on Drang."

He strode away, heading down the road.

Dad watched him go. "Michael, remember when I told you how friendly Canadians are?"

"Yes." He'd said this two or three times. Dad was born

» 27 «

and raised in Canada, so he was pretty proud of the people up here.

"Well, Ranger Morrison is one Canuck who makes me go *yuck.*" He winked. "I guess we shouldn't get too upset. It's all just a practical joke." Dad glanced at the pigeon, then back at me. "So should I flip a coin?"

"Flip a coin? Why?"

Dad's lips twisted into a wicked grin. "To see which one of us has to clean up the bird."

"You're older. You should do it."

"No, no, no, Michael—we're on holidays together and the key word is *together.* That means we split everything fifty-fifty. Besides, I brought you out here so you could learn something about responsibility."

Responsibility? Is that what this whole trip was about? Was Dad hoping he'd have a brand new kid who behaved properly by the time the vacation was over? I crossed my arms.

Dad had no idea he'd just offended me. He magically made a coin appear in his hand and was twirling it with his fingers. It was one of those gold-colored Canadian dollars. "Heads or … " He looked at the other side. " … loon."

"Do I at least get to keep the loonie if I lose?" I asked.

Dad nodded and flipped the coin skywards.

"Heads," I mumbled as it arced through the air. Dad caught the coin, slapped it on his arm, then turned to display it. A floating loon stared at me. I'd lost. Just another sign of my bad luck. He tossed me the dollar and I stuffed it in my pocket.

"Well, I'm going for my jog," Dad announced. "See you in a few minutes."

"What should I use to pick it up?"

"I'm sure you'll find something," he shouted. He was already at the edge of our campsite, pumping his knees up and down in a slow jog. "You've got a knack for being clever."

"I got it from Mom," I yelled, but he was gone, his feet a blur beneath him.

It took me awhile to choose the right instrument for the job. I finally settled on the small silver shovel in our tool bag. I went around to the side of the tent and picked up the pigeon's head.

Its eye stared at me.

Then I carefully scooped up the body. A swarm of flies took off, buzzed around, then returned to their prize. I felt my stomach tighten and wished I could somehow do all this with my eyes closed. A few flies abandoned the bird and landed on my cheek. Their tiny legs tickled me, but I couldn't take my hands off the shovel to brush them off.

I crept over to the garbage, walking as carefully as possible. Finally I got to the can and gently dropped the pigeon inside. The flies followed.

I picked up the lid and placed it on top, whispering a small prayer. It seemed like the right thing to do.

"Bye-bye, Tweety Bird," a raspy voice said behind me.

» 6 «

I turned around, expecting to see the creeps who killed the bird.

Instead, who should be standing there but the girl from last night. Wraparound, mirrored sunglasses hid her eyes, making her look like a Star Trek crew member. She wore ankle-high hiking boots, blue jean shorts and a black shirt scrawled with the words: *Reality stinks and so do you.* She was smaller than I remembered and she appeared fit. Energy seemed to crackle out from somewhere deep inside her. She smirked, then asked, "Poor little bird fall down dead?"

"Uh … yeah." Flustered, I opened my mouth again and out came: "It wasn't your bird, was it?"

I could've whacked myself on the head. What a stupid thing to say.

She stared at me, or I think she was staring because I couldn't see her eyes behind the reflective lenses. Her grin changed into a grimace.

Oh, good job, I thought. You've gone and made her mad.

"You've never been here before, have you," she said.

"No, I haven't."

She removed her shades. Her eyes glittered with humor

and I sighed in relief. "Hey, welcome to Drang Island," she said, spreading her arms like a tour guide, "the weirdest island in the whole, wide world." She stepped up and offered her hand. "By the way, thanks for the help last night. Sorry I was so defensive. I get that way when people sneak up on me in the dark. My name's Fiona Gavin."

"I'm Michael Asmundson." We shook. It felt a little awkward; I didn't quite get my hand all the way into hers. A sissy handshake. "So I … uh … see that your hair's red. Are you a Norj or a Swede or something?"

"A Norj? What's that? Some kinda nerd?"

"No, it's short for Norwegian."

She shook her head. "I'm Canadian. Born and raised in beautiful B.C. And I get the red hair from my mom. She's part Irish. Not that it's really your business."

"Sorry … I didn't mean to be snoopy."

"No harm done," Fiona said, rather matter-of-factly. She glanced past me at our campsite. "Looks like someone tried to redecorate your tent, too."

"Was yours hit?"

She nodded. "Yep, some kind of messy circular mark. If someone's going to be a graffiti bandit, they should try and pick up some artistic skills first. At least you can make out words on yours. It seems to say, 'You are marked dead.' It's like a threat or something."

"Yeah, but what does it mean? Who would write that?"

Fiona shrugged. "Who knows. Most people who do this stuff are just pimply-faced geeks, out to get a thrill. I don't imagine it'll get solved. There's only one ranger on the island."

"We met him," I told her.

"Great guy, isn't he?" She made a face like she'd just bit

into a lemon. "There's not much he can do about the vandals but stamp his feet and huff and puff. There *are* a few wild ones who hang out on Drang. Me included." She winked. I almost blushed. "Of course, maybe it's some of the sheep-stealin' hermits in the bush, claiming their territory."

"Sheep stealers? What do you mean?"

"Last year a rich sheep herder tried to raise about thirty sheep here. Thought this'd be the perfect place to graze. Cost him a lot to ship them over. They all disappeared. People think it might have been the hermits, stocking up on their mutton."

"You seem to know a lot about Drang."

"Drang's my getaway place."

"Are you here alone?"

Fiona narrowed her eyes. "What's it to you?"

"I'm a secret agent," I answered flippantly, "It's my job to ask questions." I remembered how the weather had been the night before. "You arrived after us. How did you get here?"

"Kayak."

"You came in a kayak? Through all that wind and lightning?"

"The sky was clear when I left; the storm hit me about halfway across. Kayaks are pretty dependable. And the trip wasn't that tough 'cause I was angry and I paddle better when I'm angry." I must have looked confused by her whole story, so she added, "I didn't have that far to go. My parents have a cabin on an island south of Drang."

"Do they know you're here?"

"You don't know when to stop asking questions, do you?" She looked like she was about to get real mad.

"Sorry," I whispered, and shut my mouth.

An uncomfortable silence passed between us. Then

Fiona pointed and asked, "Are those your bikes?"

"Yeah," I told her as we walked over to them. "They're rentals."

"They look pretty rugged." She lifted one up and let the front wheel drop down, catching it on the second bounce. "Good shocks on this baby."

"That's mine. I named it Sleipnir, after Odin's eight-legged horse. He was the fastest in all the worlds."

"You named your bike after a horse?" She frowned.

"Uh. Well, yeah. In our family we name everything we travel on or in; it's kind of a Viking tradition. Our boat is called Verdandi, after one of the fates; our car is Hugi and it's named for a giant who ran really fast. Well, fast as the speed of thought. Our car isn't that speedy though, so it's kind of a sarcastic joke to call it Hugi …" I trailed off.

Fiona had her hands on her hips, staring at me like I was a lunatic. "How … uh … interesting," she said. "Is the rest of your family as … uh … interesting as you?"

I opened my mouth to answer, but was distracted by the sound of someone running down the road behind us. I turned to see Dad huffing and puffing, taking his last few steps into the campsite. His t-shirt was soaked and a thin sheen of sweat glistened on his face. He was losing some of his hair and it made his forehead shine like a polished pink bowling ball. I'd learned a long time ago not to tease him about his receding hairline.

Why'd he have to go for such a short run today of all days?

He stopped in front of us. The lenses on his glasses were slightly fogged up and he was grinning mischievously. Fiona introduced herself. Dad said *hi* and raised one finger, as if he was about to start an important speech.

I knew he'd spit out something that would embarrass me. He always did whenever he found me with girls my age. He usually said things like "Michael has a birthmark on his behind" or "I hear my son's a good kisser."

Instead, he asked, "You two thinking of going biking?"

"Can we?" I blurted. "I mean—you don't mind if we borrow yours?"

"Go ahead." He took off his specs and started wiping them clean. He squinted at me. "You and I can go out tomorrow. Or the next day. We've got two weeks here."

"Do you want to go for a ride?" I asked Fiona.

"Yeah, sure," she answered, coolly. "But how about tomorrow? I was planning on taking my kayak out this morning."

"Oh … okay." I tried to hide my disappointment.

"I was hoping you'd come with me," she added, much to my surprise. "I know you can rent kayaks down at the dock. You ever been on one?"

"Yeah, a couple of times back home. Never out in the ocean, though. I'd be glad to tag along."

"Good!" Dad slipped his glasses back on. "I'll be rid of Michael for the morning at least." He winked at me, then said, "We still haven't had breakfast. You want something to eat, Fiona? Or are you gonna eat with your parents?"

Fiona glanced furtively from me to Dad. "Uh … no thanks. About breakfast, that is. I'll get some food at the tent and be back in about twenty minutes."

As I watched her leave, I thought about telling Dad that she was alone on the island, but bit my tongue. It really wasn't my business. And I sure didn't want Fiona upset with me.

"She seems nice," Dad said. "She from around here?"

"From one of the islands to the south, I think."

Dad nodded, rubbed his hands together. "How about scrambled eggs, Michael? And an orange or two?"

It sounded fine. He lit our one-pot camping stove and within a few minutes we were munching away on partly burnt eggs and bread toasted almost black.

"I can't imagine living here in the old days," Dad said. "It's fine today, in the middle of summer. But winter must have frozen the hearts of the settlers. Rain and snow and rain and snow. There are abandoned settlements on islands all around this part of B.C. Swedes, Finns, Icelanders, Danes; tough people, from a tough climate. And still they were beaten by this land—their bones buried in the earth or at the bottom of the ocean. And Drang is supposed to be the harshest of all the islands."

"Fiona said a few people actually do live here year round."

"Not many, I bet. A lone woodsman with a wood stove, a winterized cabin and plenty of survival skills could make it, but you won't find any families out here. Even the ranger packs up in October and takes a ferry to Port Hardy."

"Does Harbard live on Drang?"

Dad shrugged. "I wouldn't be surprised. He seems the type. Sometime today or tomorrow I'll see if I can track him down. Trade him a drink for a few stories. I can always just wait by the docks until he shows up."

Dad stuffed his backpack with pens, paper and note-books. "Don't go too far out in the water. And don't be trying to show off, okay?"

"What's that supposed to mean?" I muttered.

"I'm just asking you to be safe. You have been known to do stupid things to impress your friends, right?"

He was talking about the car incident again. He'll still be talking about it on his hundredth birthday.

"I'll be as careful as I can," I promised. Apparently this was enough for Dad. He hiked his pack up over his shoulder and in a few moments he'd disappeared down the road.

I cleaned up our garbage, then plopped myself down on the bench next to the tent, sipping away at my water bottle. I felt tired, like I'd run a marathon or stayed up late cramming for an exam. I reminded myself I really hadn't had the best sleep the night before. And my short conversation with Dad was echoing around my skull. It seemed he was always expecting the worst from me.

A breeze rustled the branches of a nearby tree. I looked at the thick trunk and down at the roots, which were partly uncovered. In the Old Norse stories there was a tree called Yggdrasill that went from the underworld to heaven. Its branches held up the sky and a mighty eagle sat on its topmost bough, with a hawk resting on his brow. At the tree's roots was the dragon Nidhogg: corpse eater. Yggdrasill would survive Ragnarok; even outlast the gods. Whenever I looked at any big tree, I couldn't help but think it was somehow related to the world tree.

I thought about Harbard still believing that all the gods and giants were alive. That the great wolf Skoll chased the sun down every night, and Hati, another wolf, pursued the moon. That Jormungand was sleeping in the water, waiting for the end of the world when he would rise and spew venom across the skies and earth. And what about all the ghosts and trolls that my grandpa was always harping about? Did Harbard also think they existed? How could anyone believe that? And yet last night, in the middle of the storm, I would have believed anything. If I'd been told that Thor was battling with the giants, causing all the waves and lightning, I would've said, "Of course he is. It's the only thing that makes sense."

I thought of my sister. If there's any other fourteen-year-old kid who knows her Icelandic heritage as well as I do, it's her. She would love this place. In some ways it was too bad that we both couldn't come along on this trip.

"Wake up, sleepyhead!" Fiona exclaimed from behind me. I almost jumped out of my skin. I tried to pretend she hadn't surprised me. "You must be the dreamy type," she added.

"You must be the type to sneak up on people."

"It's my specialty. Quiet as a cat and twice as fast. You ready for an ocean adventure?"

I nodded and got up. We made our way through the campground, past the Park Office and down to the docks. We saw only two other campers. "It's getting busy down here," Fiona said, sarcastically. "Can hardly get through the crowds." I laughed.

I rented a kayak, a life jacket and a double-bladed paddle from a grumpy old man who had a little shack next to the pier. He gave me back fifty cents and both quarters were dated before World War Two. Maybe it'd been awhile since he'd had a customer.

Fiona's kayak was sleek and red, shining with new paint and sitting lightly on the water. It must have been worth quite a bit of money, so I couldn't help but wonder how rich her parents were. She got in. I found my kayak a little farther along the dock. The blue paint had been scratched and it looked like it had been torpedoed and put back together again, minus a few pieces. And yet when I climbed inside, pulled the spraydeck tight and headed out into the bay, I knew I was in a good kayak.

"I think I'll call it Mjollnir, after Thor's hammer," I said, "'cause it cuts through the waves so cleanly."

Fiona rolled her eyes. She was only a few feet across from me, expertly dipping her paddle in and out of the water. "You know, your family needs help. There's more to life than Norse stories."

"Don't tell my grandpa that," I said. "He'd keel over. Or swear at you in Icelandic. My dad might even do the same."

"Did you tell him I was here by myself?" Fiona asked quietly. I thought about how I'd been tempted. "Did you?" she asked, a little louder.

I shook my head. "I didn't figure it was any of my business. I figured you'd tell him if you wanted to. I'm assuming you're not in any trouble … are you?"

She paddled a few strokes before she answered. "No, I just need a break from everything. That's all. End of story."

I wanted to ask more, to find out what she needed a break from, but I didn't have the guts to open my mouth. Besides, I hoped maybe she'd tell me on her own.

Just as we were nearing the end of the bay, Harbard passed us in his ferry. There were two people standing at the back, holding the side and gaping at the rugged cliffs of Drang. They looked a little frightened. I wondered if he'd told them that only one passenger would return. Maybe it was some sort of traditional ferryman's joke.

He stared at Fiona and me as he went past.

"He's giving us the evil eye," Fiona whispered. Then she added with a raspy laugh, "We're doomed to crash into the rocks or get blown out to sea."

"Don't say that! He probably has the power to make it happen."

"I bet he does. Everyone in this area knows ol' Harbard. They say he's got second sight. He can even talk to spirits— you know—that channeling stuff."

"Really?"

"That's what they say. I don't believe in it myself."

"I do," I admitted.

"What?" Fiona set her paddle across the keel of her kayak. "You do?"

"Well … I've seen a ghost before."

"Oh, please."

"No … I mean it. One night about five years ago, my Grandma Gunnora appeared in my room. She told me she was going on a journey, but that she'd see me again some-day. I thought it was really her, that she'd driven all the way down to Missouri to talk to me. But an hour later the whole family was awakened by the phone. It was Grandpa telling us that she had passed away in her sleep. Back in Canada."

"That's a little spooky. Did you tell anyone about her visit?"

"My sister, Sarah. No one else … except you that is."

I expected her to make fun of me, but instead Fiona just nodded and began paddling again. "Thanks for trust-ing me," she said a short time later. We were just outside the bay and the water was growing rougher. I had to work harder to move forward.

We went along the south side of the island, dwarfed by the tall cliffs. Gliding along silently, we kept our distance from the shore, where the waves smashed against solid rock. Occasionally Fiona would point something out, an inter-esting rock formation or an osprey cutting through the air.

We didn't see any other bays or places to land.

I watched Fiona out of the corner of my eye. Her skill was impressive; every movement was smooth and perfect, like she'd spent her whole life in a kayak. Now that I'd seen her on the water, I wasn't surprised at all that she'd made it through the storm the previous night.

After an hour or so, I found myself getting dog-tired. I pulled up my paddle and Fiona did the same. The waves rocked us back and forth. "Where is it you live again?" I asked.

She pointed toward open water. "That way."

"I don't see land."

"It's there, I guarantee it. Straight south, paddle till your arms feel like they're gonna fall off, then go a little farther." She rubbed her biceps. "Speaking of arms falling off, I'm about ready to head back. How about you?"

"You took the words right out of my mouth," I said.

I slipped my paddle into the water and hit something solid. Which surprised me, because we were about a hundred yards from land. I poked my paddle down again. About a foot into the water, it stopped. "The water's really shallow," I said. "There are rocks right here."

Fiona looked over the side. "There can't be. They'd be marked by buoys to warn boats." She stuck her paddle in and it would go no farther than a few inches. "Gee, you're right."

The water was too murky to really see anything. I leaned closer, almost far enough to tip the kayak. It seemed something was moving below our boats. An enormous, dark green shape. Suddenly a long smooth back, ridged with pointy vertebrae, broke the water between our kayaks, then disappeared.

"Did you see that?" I asked quickly, trying not to panic. "There's something right under us! What is it?"

"I don't know," Fiona whispered, as if she was afraid of waking it up. "Just stop poking it. We've got to get back to the bay."

She didn't have to tell me twice. I turned my kayak around, bumping the creature again with my paddle. How big was this thing? Then I pushed off and paddled madly away. I looked back after a few minutes and the water was still.

"It must have been a whale," Fiona said, sounding excited. "Can you believe it? We were that close to a whale!"

I was still gasping uncontrollably. "I thought it might be game over for us if it came to the surface."

"A whale wouldn't sink us on purpose. I wonder what kind it was?" She dug her paddle in and expertly spun her kayak so she was facing back the other way. I stopped paddling and struggled to turn my kayak. "It should surface again. They have to surface to breathe."

We watched the area for a full five minutes, but didn't see any more signs of giant mammal life. "I don't think it's around anymore," I said.

We started back to the bay. By the time we arrived I was pretty tired. Fiona was huffing a bit, too. I wouldn't admit it to her, but I was happy to have the dock beneath my feet.

When I returned the paddle and my life jacket, Fiona told the man we'd seen a whale. He looked at us like we were lunatics. "Whales don't come to this island anymore," he said. He had a smoker's raspy voice. "Not since something started eating them."

"What would do that?" I asked.

"Don't know, exactly. But I bet it wasn't a whale you saw, it was something else. Probably Drang's very own sea monster. People round here have been spotting it for ages."

» 8 «

"What a nut!" Fiona spun her finger in a circle next to her temple, the international sign for craziness. We were already a good hundred yards from the dock, well out of the old man's hearing. "There's gotta be something in the air out here that makes everyone zany."

"Yeah, he must be Harbard's cousin or something." I held my stomach. "I thought I was going to bust a gut right in front of him."

"We shouldn't laugh too hard," Fiona warned.

"Why?"

"Maybe he was right about the monster. Maybe it was the Son of Sisutl," she whispered, a wry smile on her face.

"What? Who?"

"Just a joke. The Natives in this area tell a story about Sisutl, a mighty snake with two heads, one on each end of its body. It could bring either great power or sudden death to any who encountered it. There's an old story that the Son of Sisutl, a gigantic sea serpent, still patrols this area, gobbling up lost sailors. My mom illustrated a children's book about it. The author cut out the gory parts and made the snake into a nice guy. But every island out here says they have a sea monster. They get more tourists that way."

We walked back to my campsite. "Um ... we're still gonna bike tomorrow, right?" Fiona asked. She seemed kind of hesitant, like she expected I might say no.

"Sure," I said. "I'm all for it."

"I'll see you then." She headed off to her tent. I watched her go, her red head bobbing up and down. This was turning out to be a great day. I opened the flap to our tent and went inside.

Dad was snoozing, his journal lying open on his chest. He popped one eye open. "Okay, you caught me. I just needed a nap. The walking wore me out, I guess. How'd the kayaking go?"

"We had fun. Saw what the island looked like in the daylight. And we ..." I paused. I didn't want to tell him about the whale. Knowing him, he'd overreact and say I couldn't go out again.

"And you what?"

"And then we came back. And here I am." I dropped down on my sleeping bag next to him.

"Well, I'm glad you had fun. I talked to a few locals and asked them whether they'd been bothered by vandals. They said it was the first time they'd ever heard of anyone writing on tents."

"Did they think it was kids?"

"Seemed the most likely culprits. I yacked at Harbard, too. He's busy today, but tomorrow he said he'd meet with me and tell me the whole history of the island. It took a lot of convincing, though. He's not really the social type." Dad sat up, gave me a serious look. "Did you sleep okay?"

I wondered if he'd seen me go outside during the night, if he was waiting for me to confess to it. "Yeah, I slept fine."

"I didn't. I had quite a few nightmares. I remember one

where I was still on the ferry, trying to bring it to shore myself, but I never seemed to even get close." So he'd had bad dreams, too. I was just going to tell him about my own when Dad dropped a bombshell. "Maybe they were caused by guilt."

"Guilt?" I said. This had really come out of left field. "What do you mean?"

"Well, I know you've had a tough time this last year. Your marks kinda prove that. I've been wondering if maybe it has something to do with me being gone so much. April to September is, well, half the year; so I feel like I've missed half your life. I just haven't been there for you."

I was floored, unsure of what to say or of what I was feeling. "Uh … it's okay, Dad. You made it to most of my basketball games … before I quit the team, that is."

Dad looked dejected. "I just don't do enough and I'm sorry. That's part of the reason I wanted to have this holiday with you. I'd hoped we could reconnect. I'm glad you found this new friend, but save some time for your old man, too."

So that's why he'd brought me on the trip, to get back in touch. "I will," I promised.

"Good." It looked like Dad was about to hug me, but I wasn't quite ready for that. I stopped giving out hugs when I was a kid. A moment of slightly uncomfortable silence passed. I couldn't think of anything to say.

"Let's make some lunch," Dad suggested. We did. Hot dogs and beans. Later we went for a walk, following the trails east of the campground. We didn't talk much, but there was something nice about just spending time with Dad. Although, I have to admit, I did find myself thinking about Fiona often.

That night I slept soundly. I didn't have any nightmares. It was almost like a normal vacation.

» 9 «

Fiona showed up just after we were done breakfast. Dad had already left to find Harbard, though not before he made me promise not to bike too far into the woods. He'd heard from one of the locals that it would probably rain today. As far as I understood it, that was just normal weather in B.C.

"Aren't you ready yet?" were the first words out of Fiona's mouth. "I don't like to be kept waiting. I'm a type A personality."

"What does the A stand for? Abnormal? Or abrasive?"

"Oh, aren't you the funny one. It stands for 'About to go biking by myself.'"

"Kinda touchy, aren't you?" I filled my bottle at the tap and fastened it in the holder on my bike. "Don't worry, maybe later I can teach you a few *good* comebacks." Fiona stood there with her arms crossed, looking steamed. I chuckled and ducked into the tent. I came out with my biking gloves, my fanny pack, and my pride and joy: a black Nutech helmet with flames down the sides. I zipped up the tent.

"You gonna wear a sissy brain bucket?" Fiona asked. It didn't sound like a joke.

I glanced down at my helmet. I felt like dropping it on the ground and saying *naw, I was just kidding ha ha*. But I remembered a rather gory film we were shown at school once about head injuries. I won't go into details; I'll just say that I never wanted my head to look like a squashed watermelon.

"I wanna keep the few wits I still have inside my skull," I told Fiona.

"Where's it you come from again?"

"Missouri."

"Do they make you wear those things down there?"

"Nope." I paused. "I just want to."

She raised both her hands, palms up, and shrugged. "Hey, whatever, it's a free country." She quickly lowered the seat on Dad's bike. Then she pulled her sunglasses from her back pocket, slipped them over her eyes, jumped on the bike and jammed down on the pedal. Dirt shot from under the wheel and she launched onto the road. "Catch me if you can!"

I followed as fast as I could. A few hundred yards later, Fiona cut up a path. She didn't slow down for at least twenty minutes, heading over jumps, up and down sharp trails, most of them riddled with stones and roots that rattled my brain as I went pounding over them. It took all my energy to keep up with her. Thankfully, I'd done quite a bit of biking back in Chillicothe.

And my bike, Sleipnir, was perfect, even better than the expensive one I had at home. It responded to every bump like it had a mind of its own and knew exactly where it wanted to go. At one point I took a jump and thought I'd lost control, but when I landed the bike stayed balanced.

We were getting to be a long ways away from the campground. I thought about my promise to Dad to stay nearby, but there was no way I was going to ask Fiona to turn around. No way.

The path took us through a dense clump of gnarled trees that blocked out the sunlight. The farther along we went, the thicker the trunks became. Many of them had been around for hundreds and hundreds of years. They were so high I couldn't see the top. Not that I really tried; I didn't dare take my eyes off the track.

The shade was cool and the only thing that kept me warm was pedaling. Fiona showed no sign of slowing down. She dipped in and out of holes, weaving off the path and back on again. Once she came so close to a tree that her handlebars grazed it, chipping the bark. Then she zipped away, laughing. Wasn't she afraid of anything?

She was still wearing her sunglasses, even in this darkened area. It was a wonder she hadn't planted herself face first in the ground yet.

A short time later we broke through the bush onto an abandoned, mostly overgrown road. "They must have logged here," Fiona yelled, then she followed it. I was a few yards behind. The trail had two separate tracks and was wide enough that it felt safe to look around. The trees were getting so large I imagined their roots digging down into underground lakes. Their branches formed a tunnel above us.

Suddenly I sensed something moving to my left. Keeping pace with me. I blinked; wondered if it was a trick of the shadows. Or a deer? Or coyote?

I slowed, stared. There it was again. A dark shape, bounding through the underbrush, rustling the leaves and branches. I stopped and squinted, trying to spot it once more. A pine cone rolled out into the open. I padded up to where it had come out.

Fiona had pulled up about fifty yards away. "What are you doing?"

"I thought I saw something."

She spun quickly around and wheeled back to where I stood. "What?"

"There's an animal in the trees." I pointed. The leaves were shaking.

"I don't see anything."

I leaned down and peered into the bush. I remembered the thing that had crossed my path the night of the storm. "I could swear I caught a glimpse of eyes. Are there any animals on this island about the size of a cat?" I asked.

"Not that I know of. Are you sure it's not your imagination?"

"I saw something!" I crept forward until I had a clear view of the area where I had last seen signs of movement. There was nothing but a patch of empty ground. "At least I think I did." I shivered. Now that we had stopped moving, I was cooling down. Fast.

"It was probably a rabbit," Fiona offered. "Let's get going. Maybe there's some open space ahead where the sun'll warm us up. I'm freezing."

Fiona sped down the trail again and I struggled to keep pace. She turned a minute later and headed up another thin path lined with trees. I stopped and glanced back the way we'd come.

Sunlight barely penetrated the branches, making the leaves glow yellow and green. A black shape, about the size of a small dog, shot across the road and disappeared. It moved so fast I couldn't tell what it was.

I shook my head. It was probably twice as scared of us as we were of it. At least that's what I hoped. I waited for another couple of moments, but I didn't see a thing.

» 10 «

Fiona chose a path that was uphill, steep and winding, so I really had to get up off the seat to push the pedals down. My legs started to burn, and still we climbed higher and higher. When we finally reached the top, she stopped.

I pulled up behind her. We were in a clearing, high on a hill. Below us was the wide open ocean. No other islands could be seen, only the shimmering blue water, endless and looking like it would be impossible to cross. The sun was behind us, so I knew I must be looking west onto the Pacific.

One section of the island jutted out into the water, giving us a clear view of its edges. There were sheer cliff walls that dropped forty or fifty feet down to the water. Drang was really a natural fortress, like Alcatraz on steroids.

Large birds circled around the rocks, occasionally diving down into the ocean to catch unsuspecting fish. Waves smashed up against Drang's side.

I undid my water bottle and took a sip. Fiona did the same.

Peering down the hill, I spotted a small log cabin. It had a sod roof and was surrounded by about twelve obelisks placed in a semicircle, each about half as high as the cabin. They were like a partially completed wall, meant to protect the home. How on earth had they been carried there?

A vegetable garden was growing near the edge of the cliffs. It looked to be healthy and full of green plants, but we weren't close enough to see what kind. Three thin scarecrows stood guard, shirts flapping in the wind.

"Who do you suppose lives there?" I asked, pointing out the cabin to Fiona.

"You want to sneak down and take a look?"

"Not on your life."

Fiona laughed. "They don't make 'em too brave in Missouri, do they?"

"They don't make us stupid either," I retorted.

Fiona's laugh grew louder and I could feel myself getting really angry. Who did this girl think she was? I thought of how my ancestors, like Grettir the Strong, would never let anyone make fun of them. I got off Sleipnir, kicked the kickstand down, let the bike go and started stomping toward the cabin.

Fiona stopped laughing. "Where are you going?" she shouted after me.

"Where do you think?" I undid my helmet and latched it to my belt.

"Hey … I was just kidding …" Suddenly her tone became urgent. "Get down! Hide!"

"What?" I stopped.

She was pointing frantically at the cabin. "Someone's there!" She had taken off her sunglasses to get a better look.

I knelt. A man was limping out into the open, next to the garden. His hair was gray and wild.

I snuck back up the hill to Fiona. "It's Harbard," I said.

"I can see that. I didn't know this was where he lived.

He's one of the few who actually stay on Drang year round. He's half Viking and half Native, you know."

"Half what?"

"Indian. His tribe used to live here. A long time ago, before the rest of us came. His dad was some Scandinavian or Icelander, but his mom was from the Kwakiutl tribe."

"Where's his tribe now?"

"Dunno. Guess they got smart and left."

Harbard began hoeing his garden. He seemed pretty harmless. "Is this his land? Is he going to be mad that we're here?"

"What he doesn't know won't hurt him," Fiona said, bravely. "Though we should probably be careful. There's a rumor he catches stray kids and boils them up for stew."

"What? Get real!"

Fiona laughed. "Just kidding. I actually haven't heard anyone say anything bad about ol' Harbard."

"You almost had me going for a second there. You're not bad at pulling someone's leg. Not as good as me, of course."

This made her eyes glitter with mischief. "I bet you a dollar I can get you again. Right now."

I didn't like the sounds of this, but I wasn't going to back down. I pulled out the coin my father had given me. "You're on."

Fiona grabbed the loonie and shoved it in her pocket, saying, "I might as well have it, because I'm gonna show you who's the better trickster." She put a hand to her mouth and howled like a wolf. Loud.

"Hey!" I tried to stop her. Her cry echoed around us.

Harbard jerked his head our way. He shielded his eyes from the sun, squinted.

"What are you doing?" I barked. This was one guy I didn't want to annoy.

"He's not the fastest runner in the world. We can be gone before he gets anywhere near us."

"You're crazy!"

"Oh, don't be such a … uh oh."

Harbard had made his way to the woodpile. He was now holding a large axe. "*Draugr!*" he yelled. "*Fardur burt!*" He grabbed the chain around his neck with his free hand. Was he trying to ward us away? Did he think we were evil spirits? Fetches? "*Galdrakarl! Flya!*"

Then he whistled, sharply. A long, black hound slipped out of the cabin, ears pricked up. It was the biggest dog I'd ever seen. It could probably bring down a deer on its own. Harbard snarled a command.

"We better get outta here," Fiona whispered. She didn't sound as brave as she had just a minute ago. "Fast."

The dog stared in our direction. Then began loping toward us.

In a heartbeat I was on my bike and pedaling like a maniac. I glanced back to see Fiona right behind me. We went up a few feet then down into a gully, trees blurring past. I didn't care which direction we traveled. I just wanted to put as much space as possible between Harbard's dog and us.

We took a long loop on a thin winding path, then twisted back and forth. By this time I was wondering if I'd ever find my way home to the campground.

I glanced back. There didn't seem to be anything following us.

We headed up another hill. The way was getting even rougher and some of the stones looked sharp enough to puncture my tires. We climbed higher and then sped down into a valley that was crammed with long, green grass that hid a lot of oversized, jagged rocks. The sun beat down; sweat dripped into my eyes, blurring my vision.

The path dipped steeply. My stomach lurched and I grabbed tight onto the bike, praying it would bounce across the stones beneath us, hoping I could somehow manage to stay on. I wasn't even wearing my helmet. It was still strapped to my belt. If I fell here I'd be torn to shreds, all the bones in my body broken.

We were now rattling our way across flat, stony ground. The whole area had been smoothed out like a river bed.

Suddenly there was nothing but empty space in front of us. I slammed on my brakes. Fiona ground to a halt a yard or two behind.

We were on the edge of a deep ravine that stretched in either direction as far as the eye could see. It was as if the whole earth had cracked open, dividing the island in two. The chasm was fifty feet wide in some places and only about ten in others. Below us was a drop of a hundred feet or more. Sunlight didn't penetrate far enough to illuminate the bottom. All we could see was a swirl of mist and gloom.

It took me a second to catch my breath. I was glad to see Fiona was winded, too.

"I had no idea this was here," she spat out between gulps of air. "I wonder how far it goes?"

I shrugged. I scanned the open area behind us. There was no trace of the dog.

"I'm sorry," Fiona said.

"What for?"

"For … for playing that trick on Harbard. Getting us in trouble. I sometimes do things without really thinking first. It was dumb."

I opened my mouth to say *yeah, it was really dumb,* but the look of genuine sadness on her face stopped me. "Well … it's alright. We seem to be okay."

"Yeah, except I dropped my sunglasses. That dog's probably chewing on them as we speak." She glanced up. "At least there are a few clouds in the sky now. I won't be squinting all the time."

"Well, we can't go back that way. I hope we can find another path home."

"That shouldn't be much of a problem. There are lots of trails out here." She pointed in a direction I believed was east. "Maybe if we push our bikes toward those trees we'll find another way, though I'm not quite up to the long ride back yet. Mind if we find some place to sit for awhile?"

"Good idea," I said. We headed across a flat space, carpeted with grass and stones. We were only a few feet from the chasm. I kept looking down, enthralled by the depth of the hole.

After a few minutes of walking, Fiona motioned in front of us. "See that?"

I nodded. A hulking, ancient pine had fallen across a place where the crevice wasn't that wide, forming a bridge. We neared. Ashes surrounded the splintered remains of the trunk. It still smelled of fire.

"I bet this got hit when that storm came through," I said. "There was some pretty wicked lightning."

The whole area looked familiar to me, almost like I'd been here before, or at least seen it. It was the weirdest feeling, since this was my first visit to Drang.

Fiona kicked back her kickstand and left her bike standing next to the stump. She grabbed onto a branch and climbed up the fallen tree. She held out her arms for balance, padded back and forth, then did a graceful pirouette and bowed. She stood with her hands on her hips, looking like a female Indiana Jones. "You know, I wonder if anyone else has even walked on that side of the island. We could be the first. You up for it?"

I remembered my promise to Dad. I knew we were a long way from camp right now, that if anything happened Dad would have a tough time finding us.

Fiona was staring at me. "I can't stand around all day," she said.

As long as I was careful, nothing would go wrong. And besides, sooner or later I had to take charge of my own life. I gave the tree the once-over. It was long and thick and seemed to be sitting pretty solid. It didn't look that dangerous.

"Okay," I said, finally, "let's go."

With some difficulty I climbed up. I gulped some air and led the way across, picking my way past branches, being careful to step right in the middle of the tree, not on the sides where the bark was loose. When we were about half way across, I decided to look down. Dark, pointed cliff walls and sharp rocks beckoned to me. They spun in my vision. A thin, silver line of water glistened in the depths.

I stepped too far to one side and slipped.

» 11 «

"Here! Grab on!" Fiona was lying on her stomach, reaching down.

I clung to a thick branch, my feet dangling in empty air below me. "I can't reach!"

She moved a little closer. The branch started to creak. I couldn't pull myself any higher, so I kicked out with my foot, found the edge of the tree and pushed up.

We linked hands and with her help I climbed to the center of the fallen tree. I sucked in enough air to fill a zeppelin.

"You gonna live?" Fiona asked.

"Yeah," I said, once I'd calmed down and stopped feeling like throwing up. It took everything I had just to stand. My legs were wobbly and I didn't trust them anymore.

Fiona was right behind me. "Don't look down until you get to the other side. It makes it easier."

Now she tells me, I thought. I concentrated on my footing. We slowly moved along the trunk, using the tree branches for balance. It took a lifetime and then some to get to the other side. I was sure my hair had gone gray.

We jumped down. Fiona rubbed her hands together. "We better get back before nightfall. I'd hate to cross that in the dark."

I didn't want to cross it again at all. "What time is it now?" I asked after noticing that my watch was missing from my wrist. It was likely still sitting in the tent, next to my sleeping bag.

Fiona shrugged. "I don't wear a watch in the summer. But it's sometime around twelve or so, I'd guess. Enough time to take a gander around this place and get back for hot dogs. Which reminds me, did you happen to bring anything to eat?"

I dug in my fanny pack, came up with two pieces of beef jerky, a granola bar and a caramel candy. We split everything, except the candy. I bowed deeply and offered it to her, saying, "Sweets for the sour."

"I hope you enjoy your joke, 'cause I'm gonna enjoy the candy." Grinning, Fiona snatched the candy out of my hand.

It felt kind of nice to make her smile. We sat in the open on two bench-sized stones and ate. Didn't say too much. I watched birds arcing through the sky.

Fiona stretched out her legs and sighed. "So what's Missouri like?"

"Hot most of the time. We live out on a ranch near Chillicothe."

"Is your dad a rancher?"

"Kind of. Dad trains bird dogs."

"Bird dogs? Do they have wings?"

"No." For a second I wondered if she was serious; then I saw the smirk on her face. "They're dogs that hunters use. Dad comes up to Saskatchewan every year in the late spring for a few months to train them. It's just too hot and muggy in Missouri. Our hired man is doing it right now, while Dad takes a break."

"You must get sick of the barking."

"You don't even hear it after awhile." I found myself wanting to tell her about my father. "Dad's a writer. Or a collector, I guess. He likes to collect modern versions of all the Norse myths and folk tales. He has a book contract with one of the big publishers in New York. He just has to finish the last chapter. He's been working on the whole thing for three years."

"Man, that's a long time," Fiona said. She picked up a small stone and tossed it about twenty feet. It rolled into the chasm. She then looked me right in the eye and asked, "So, do you have lots of friends down there in the States?" Her eyes were a light shade of green and I gotta say I was spellbound by them. They were the kind of eyes you'd expect on a Valkyrie. Fierce, proud, perfect, glowing with —

"Hello! Earth to Michael." Fiona waved her hand in my face.

"What? What did you ask me?" I asked.

"Do you have lots of friends or do you bore them to death with long pauses in your conversations?"

"Uh … no, not too many friends. We came to Missouri two years ago and I found a couple good pals. But their fathers were laid off by a manufacturing company and forced to find work out of state. So about half way through the year they moved, and I was kind of on my own."

"I know what you're saying. I just started going to a private school in Victoria. Mom and Dad thought it would be better for me. 'Course, I didn't know a soul there."

"Well, I must admit, I'm not completely alone. I actually hang out with my sister quite a bit. We're twins."

"Really? So, tell me: if she studies for an exam, do the answers appear in your head, too?"

I laughed. "No. If they did, I'd be a straight A student. She always gets higher marks than me. Specially this year."

"It must be great to have a sister. I'm an only child."

"Really? That must be tough."

"What do you mean?" She narrowed her eyes slightly.

"Well, who do you blame your mistakes on? That's what siblings are for."

She laughed. "I just blame everything on my parents."

"I guess that works," I said. "So what do your parents do?"

"Dad's a prof at the University of Victoria. Mr. Engineer of the Year—whoopty-do." Fiona twirled her finger in the air. "And dear ol' *Mom* is a graphic artist."

"Don't you like them?"

She shook her head. "I don't have to like them, do I? Just lump them. They're kind of hard to get along with sometimes. Well, most of the time. Always telling me what to do. And I don't know if you noticed, but I'm a little headstrong. At least that's what they keep telling me." She grinned.

"Is that why you came to Drang? To get away?"

Fiona nodded. "An unplanned vacation. I had a fight with Mom over this summer school she wants me to go to. It's for musically gifted children."

"What instrument do you play?"

"Ukulele."

"Really?"

"No." Fiona gave me this look like I was about as smart as a toad. "Piano, when I'm forced to. It's what all the hoity-toities make their teen prodigies play. Or violin. Registration is this weekend, so I slipped out the back of the cabin. Mom and Dad probably won't notice I'm gone until they call for me to get in the car. I'll go back tomorrow and get yelled at in stern, authoritative tones."

"Won't they be looking for you?"

She shook her head. "I've done it before. Their new approach is to ignore anything bad that I do. They figure I just want attention."

"If you really want their attention, just crash your Dad's car."

"What do you mean?"

"Last winter, I told some guys on our basketball team that I drove Dad's Mustang all the time. It's a '67. I was just bragging, trying to impress them. So they dared me to bring it to practice. I did and gave a few of them a ride. But it was a wet, snowy day and the wipers weren't really working. Plus, the windshield fogged up. Next thing I knew I hit a post in the parking lot and the car got hung up on it. The guys piled out and I was left there."

"Did you wreck the car?"

"Not really, just dented the fender. And gave it a flat tire, too. It was more a trust thing. Mom and Dad didn't have much faith in me after that. Not that I was all that high on their 'People To Depend On' list before."

"I take it you don't have your license yet. How old are you, anyway?"

The question surprised me. My heartbeat quickened. "Fifteen … that is, I turn fifteen in a few days."

Fiona nodded wisely. "I remember when I turned fifteen."

"When?" How old was she?

"Two weeks ago. Mom and Dad bought me the kayak. They didn't guess I'd be using it so soon."

Just fifteen. It wouldn't be long before we'd be the same age. There was something kind of nice about that.

Without any warning, Fiona elbowed me. I almost shot straight in the air. She was squinting into the distance. "You know that animal you saw in the woods?"

"Y-yes."

"What if I told you I just spotted it?"

» 12 «

I scrambled to my feet. "What? Where?"

Fiona pointed at the tree we'd just crossed. "I saw it about half way down the trunk. It wasn't very big."

Walking as quietly as we could, we moved toward the tree, eyes peeled. We were only a few feet from the edge of the chasm. "Can you see it?"

She motioned. "There, it's in the branches, coming toward us."

Then I saw it, about thirty feet away. Or I saw something. It was there but indistinct, an ebony shape, rustling from shadow to shadow, hidden by pine needles, hardly making them wiggle. It hadn't seen us yet. As it came closer, I still couldn't tell what the creature was. It was dark and blended in with its surroundings.

We crouched near the edge of the chasm, behind the topmost branches of the fallen tree. Staring. Now our little visitor was completely hidden by green. A branch moved. A second later, a pine cone fell into the depths. Then the animal darted across an open space into more shade. It stopped about two yards away from us; didn't make a sound for a few minutes. I wondered if it had heard something. Or had it picked up our scent?

I put my finger to my lips and Fiona nodded as I grabbed a broken stick the size of a baseball bat. It had been burnt on one end.

I used it to slowly part the branches.

We peered in. Nothing. I lifted another section of needles. Something there?

I leaned closer, pushing the stick further into the branches.

And finally, there it was, the strangest creature I'd ever seen. Its hairless body seemed to shimmer, though it was dark as tar.

Two eyes narrowed. It hissed. It wasn't a cat-like sound at all.

"Michael, I think—"

The animal burst from the tree and into the air, straight at me. It grew larger, stretching taller and wider, looking almost human. I thought I could see claws and a gaping mouth riddled with teeth. I threw out my hands. The thing hit my chest, but it had no weight. Instead it seemed to pass right through me.

Its touch froze the blood in my veins. My muscles stiffened. I wobbled, then caught a stone with my heel and collapsed backwards onto the ground. Rocks jabbed my spine and my ribs. The last bit of air in my lungs whooshed out of me.

I turned my head to see the thing bounding across the plateau. It was small again and seemed to be scampering on two legs, heading at odd angles, back and forth, like it was lost. It wasn't shaped like any animal I'd ever seen. It hopped over an outcropping of stone and disappeared.

"What on earth was that?" Fiona asked.

I waited for my breath to return. Then I slowly, carefully, sat up. "I have no idea, but I don't ever want to see it again."

Fiona was standing next to me now, looking concerned. "It didn't hurt you, did it?"

"Not that I can tell." I poked at myself. To my amazement there weren't any scrapes or sore spots on my chest and arms.

She extended her hand, helped me to my feet. Her grip was warm and sure.

"It didn't even hit me," I said. "It's like it passed right through. Did you see what it looked like?"

"No, only a blur."

"Did it … did it seem to get larger, then shrink down again?"

"What?"

I rubbed the back of my head. "It changed size as it came at me."

"That's just your imagination. The thing wasn't any bigger than a cat." I wasn't sure if she was right, but I didn't want to argue any more. Fiona looked toward where it had last disappeared. "Do you think it was following our trail?"

I shrugged. "Who knows."

Then I remembered why this place looked so familiar. It had appeared in the nightmare I'd had our first night on Drang. I'd followed a specter over a fallen tree.

How could I dream something and then actually see it, days later?

I glanced at the real tree and at our bikes, waiting on the other side. Things seemed safer over there.

Fiona caught my eye. "You're not thinking of going back, are you? Not so soon. We've only been here a few minutes."

"Yeah, and look what's happened." I resisted telling her

about my nightmare. After all the Norse stuff I'd babbled about, she probably already thought I was a bit crazy.

Fiona punched my shoulder, softly. "Don't be a party pooper. Why don't we explore this direction, away from that … that … whatever it was?"

"What if there are more of them?"

"Well … we won't poke them with a stick. They'll probably just run away like that one did. C'mon, let's take a look around."

My body was still feeling stiff. It'd be good to walk some of it out, I decided. I wouldn't want to get back up on that tree bridge with aching muscles.

We headed westward across an open plain littered with smashed rocks. It looked like Thor himself could have been here, testing out his hammer. Or maybe giants had played a vicious game of Murder Ball. We picked our way around the debris. Green grass and small trees still found a way to grow, working their way in between cracks and into small patches of soil. I was glad I had good hiking boots on and equally happy when a cloud drifted between us and the sun. I'd been sweating like a pig; I hoped I didn't smell like one.

Soon the rocks grew in size and the ground sloped upwards. We squeezed by two stones that could have been brought over from Stonehenge. This part of the island was much rougher.

"I've never seen anything so desolate," Fiona said. We came to a small rise, but all that lay in front of us was more of the same.

Fiona led me down a narrow path that gradually descended a long way. It became a pass, with rocks on either side of us. We went from shade to light to shade and finally stumbled into a small ravine. Fiona turned a corner and immediately stepped back, almost into me.

"What is it?" I stopped.

She pointed at a steel pole sticking out of the ground. Next to it was a body.

Actually it was half a body.

Of a goat.

And it looked like someone had torn it in two and left just the top part. The animal was chained to a thick steel pole that jutted straight up into the air. It would have taken a pretty big guy to hammer that rod right into the rock.

A few feet behind the goat was an obelisk, similar to the ones at Harbard's except this stone was as black as a starless night. It was set flush against the rock wall. Runes were printed in red across its surface. The grass, which had managed to sprout in corners and cracks all across the ravine, was dead all around the stone.

Flies buzzed around. I caught a whiff of the carcass and felt the urge to barf.

"That's pretty gross," Fiona said, "about the grossest thing I've ever seen."

We moved upwind from the goat's body. I ran a hand through my sweat-slicked hair. The sun turned this spot into a frying pan—the day wasn't getting any cooler.

I stepped to the other side of the animal, where I found a piece of stained, woolly hide and a pile of broken bones, some small and brittle, others thick and heavy. Vines had grown around part of a rib cage, but most of the bones looked like they'd only been there for a short while. None of the remains appeared human.

"Some psycho must have tied it up and killed it," I said. "Who would do that? And why?"

Fiona shrugged. "I don't know." She bent over and poked at the piece of hide with a twig. "Doesn't this look like sheep skin? Remember those sheep that went missing? Maybe they all ended up tied to this stake."

"Kind of a *baaad* way to go," I quipped.

Fiona rolled her eyes and grimaced. "That's not even funny."

"Sorry," I said. "It's an old habit, passed down from my ancestors. Dad says the Vikings used to make jokes all the time when they were in a tight spot."

"I'm sure they were funnier."

"Probably. How about this one? This Viking guy snuck up on another guy named Thorgeir and tried to kill him with an axe, but he missed, ran away and left his weapon behind. The next time Thorgeir saw him, he planted the axe in his skull, saying, 'You forgot your axe.'"

Fiona smiled slightly. "Now that is funny."

"At least he didn't say, 'You axed for it.'"

She groaned and took a few steps away from the goat. Or me. I wasn't sure which she wanted to avoid most.

A green blur caught my eye. I focused on it, just in time to see a four-foot-long serpent slide into a hole near my feet.

"Snakes!" I exclaimed. "I just saw one."

"Yeah, that's normal." Fiona was kicking the metal pole. It didn't budge. "There are always tons of snakes on Drang. They're not dangerous. Well, except for the rattlers. If you get bit by one you just can't move around too much or you'll make the venom spread faster. My father explained the whole process to me: first you'll feel pain, then nausea, chills and dizziness. You know, all the same things you experience on a first date."

I forced a laugh. If only she knew how close she was to the truth. It was time to stick to a more comfortable topic. "Dad said this island is known for its snakes."

Fiona nodded. "Some guy named Doc Siroiska came to study them and some other odd stuff on Drang. Last year. It was a big deal 'cause he was one of them superstar scientists like David Suzuki."

"Oh, yeah," I said, pretending I knew who David Suzuki was. "What was this doctor's name again?"

"Siroiska."

"Hey, I think my dad mentioned him, too. Didn't Siroiska disappear?"

"Yeah. They figure he fell into a chasm or the water. Or got lost in a cave. They searched the whole island and the surrounding ocean. Never found a trace. Reporters said he probably wanted to vanish. Apparently he was bankrupt." She paused. "But some of the fishermen who pass by this end of the island say they hear his ghost calling out, warning people away from here. Spooky, eh?"

I looked down the snake hole. It reminded me of a ground squirrel burrow. Moist air and a smell of wet dung drifted upwards. There were probably hundreds of serpents nesting down there. I edged cautiously away, even though I knew most snakes wouldn't bite unless they were provoked.

I heard something splashing. I followed the sound, heading toward the edge of the ravine.

There was about a ten-foot drop into the water. It would have been straight down, except someone had carved out a slide from the solid rock. It looked like a stone age version of a water slide, but it was about twenty feet in width. Waves splashed against the bottom, making the swishing sound.

I called Fiona over and asked, "What do you think this is for?"

"Beats me." She knelt down and ran her hands across the top edge. "What's all this stuff?" Her fingers were covered with greenish flakes, each the size of a quarter. "It's like fish scales or something."

"The snakes probably suntan there."

"Oh yuck!" She wiped her hands together, trying desperately to clean them. "Look, these things just cling to your fingers."

The slide was worn smooth, as if something had traveled against the rocks a thousand times over. It was a fairly steep slope; one false step and we'd slip straight down.

About a hundred yards away, an immense shape broke the surface of the water, then vanished into the blue depths.

"Did you see that?" I asked.

"Yeah, maybe it was the same whale we saw yesterday. I didn't spot a fin, though."

Neither had I. I stared, waiting for it to appear again, but the ocean was calm now.

My eyes were drawn to a black mark on the side of the ravine. It was a twisting serpentine symbol that looked like a snake biting its own tail. The paint reminded me of the stuff that had been used for the graffiti on our tent.

"Jormungand," I said.

"What?"

I walked over to the image. "He's a giant snake from Norse mythology. The Vikings believed he would one day rise out of the ocean and spew venom across the earth and sky."

"Sounds pleasant. Did he ever do it?"

"Yes, but Thor was there to stop him. They'd been enemies ever since Jormungand was born. Thor fought against him three times. Once, as a trick, the giants turned Jormungand into a tiny cat and dared Thor to lift him. He did and was able to get the cat to raise one paw, which amazed the giants because he was really lifting the giant snake. Another time, when Thor was fishing with a giant called Hymir, the giant caught two whales. Thor didn't want to be outdone, so he rowed into deeper water, cast out his hook with a bull's head for bait, and snagged Jormungand. Thor actually pulled him up and tried to pound his skull in with his hammer. But before he could kill the monster, Hymir, who was scared of Jormungand, cut Thor's line. Thor and Jormungand met for the last time during Ragnarok: the final battle of the gods. Thor slew the serpent, then died from the poison."

"Kind of a tough way to go."

"Yeah, but when you're a Viking god, you gotta expect that you won't die in your sleep. Most of the gods were killed during Ragnarok, but a new world rose up from the old one, with many new courts and buildings fairer than the sun."

Fiona was giving me an odd look. If I wasn't mistaken, it was something like admiration. "You seem to know a lot about this stuff. You're smarter than I first thought."

I let her insult slip by. "I've been told these tales over and over since I was a kid. My parents are myth junkies."

"So who do you suppose painted this snake thing?"

"Dad said some Icelanders built a settlement on Drang. Maybe they did it, marking this as some kind of sacred place."

"What would they use it for?"

"Well, I'm tempted to say sacrifices, but that just doesn't make sense. Most Icelanders have been Christians for almost a thousand years."

She traced the outline of the snake with her fingers. "When was the settlement here?"

"Dad didn't know exactly. The late 1800s or so. Or maybe that's when they left. I don't remember."

Fiona pointed at the dead goat. "I've got news for you. *That* has only been here for a week at the most. It could have been killed just last night. I'd guess someone else besides the settlers has a thing for this snake. Or for chopping up livestock."

"I don't know about you," I said, not wanting to sound too frightened, "but I think it's time we headed back."

Fiona nodded. "You're right. I've had enough weirdness for one day."

Behind me, something whispered. I whipped around in time to catch a glimpse of the creature that had attacked me earlier. It disappeared into a hole atop the cliff walls.

Fiona saw it too. "Was it that thing again?"

"Yeah, but it's gone. I wish I knew why it's following us."

For the first time, Fiona looked worried. "Let's just get out, okay? I don't want to be here anymore."

I stepped over the goat and started up the path. Fiona followed close behind. After about five minutes of walking she stopped and looked back, her hands on her hips. "I don't think this is the trail we were on before."

"What makes you say that?" I asked. "I'm sure we took the right one."

"We may have started on the right one, but somewhere we took a wrong turn. I think."

"Are we going south?" I asked.

"It's hard to tell. This path is always twisting one way or the other."

"Do you think we should go back and make sure?"

She shook her head. "I don't want to see that mangled goat again. Besides, we've come this far. And maybe we are on the right track; it could just look different going this way."

We trudged on. Once or twice the sun shone down on us, but mostly it was blocked by the rocks and trees. A few clouds drifted through the sky, casting cool shadows. My body and head were still sore and I thought again about when that thing had touched me. Had it given me some disease?

Soon I grew parched and I couldn't stop myself from picturing the water bottle I'd left on my bike. What I wouldn't do to have one sip from it right now.

A noise snapped me out of my little dream. Footsteps. Loud footsteps. Just behind us. I stopped, turned, and listened for a second.

Fiona stopped too. "What is it?"

I heard a bird or two and the rustle of leaves in the breeze. "Nothing," I told her. "Just dreaming, I guess."

We climbed up another small hill and onto a plateau. There, laid out before us, were several domes made of piled rocks. The mounds were each about ten feet high. Vegetation had crept across everything, adding a green tinge to the desolate area. A few crooked trees poked their trunks up out of the dirt, looking forlorn and wasted.

"What are these?" Fiona asked, moving to the largest of the mounds, then going around the far side. I followed. There was something familiar about its shape. I'd seen one before or a picture of one. The dome was broken open, huge stones had been cracked to pieces and rolled aside, leaving a gaping hole. The inside of the mound was hollow, dark and uninviting.

And yet on some level it beckoned to me. I edged slightly

forward, not really aware that I was moving. Was there whispering coming from inside that darkness? I felt an urge to get out of the light and go inside.

I slowly stepped ahead, came right to the edge of the opening. It was colder here, but still I moved forward. Did I hear shallow, raspy breathing now? Or was it the breeze whistling through the stones?

I caught a sudden whiff of something long dead and terribly rotten.

» 14 «

The stench was thick and overwhelming. I reeled back and coughed, covering my mouth. My stomach tightened. I felt like I was about to be sick.

"What's wrong?" Fiona asked. She rested her hand on my shoulder.

I shook my head. "It stinks inside," I said, hoarsely. I stumbled a few feet away and examined the dome warily. Rain and wind had worn the rocks down.

Now I knew exactly what these were, had seen a hundred pictures of them in books on Scandinavian history. "These are cairns: burial mounds." I cleared my throat. "And I think they're pretty old. It looks like thieves got into this one."

"Is this how the settlers would've buried their dead?" Fiona asked. Her voice was a little shaky.

"Maybe." I glanced around. I edged nearer to the opening of the cairn, wanting a better look at the stones. "But there aren't any crosses or markings. Most people would want you to know who was buried here. My ancestor, Grettir the Strong, used to go into cairns like this and fight the ghouls who lived inside."

"Yeah, right," she said. The way she rolled her eyes made me smile.

"Okay, so the stories are mostly made up, but you've got to give the Icelanders credit for their superior imaginations. According to the sagas, Grettir would go inside the cairn, kill the monster and come out with all the treasure. And there was lots of treasure. The greatest chieftains were often buried with their wealth, even with their horses sometimes."

I shuffled a little to one side. The sun was coming from the wrong direction to allow light into the mound, so I couldn't see the interior clearly. Despite that, an object glinted in the darkness. "Looks like the thieves missed something," I said. I moved in closer, holding my breath, wondering if I had spotted an axe or a medallion.

"Don't go in there!"

Fiona's voice startled me. "Why?"

She looked pale. "Someone dead once slept there ... or still is. Just let them rest. It's giving me the creeps."

The glittering blinked out, then reappeared. It was a circular light, almost like an eye. It vanished again. I edged away. "You're right. Besides, it would probably bring me bad luck."

Fiona's face was tight with worry. "Let's find our way home," I said.

We hurried to the end of the plateau and followed another path that lead to higher ground. We climbed higher; patches of grass appeared.

We walked briskly for another ten minutes. Finally, the landscape opened up. We stopped at the top of a rise. The sun was about three quarters of the way through the sky. The heat took some of the chill from my bones. Fiona leaned against a ledge. "Let's have a rest. I'm exhausted."

I inhaled, filling my lungs. Fresh air helped drive away the fear I was feeling only minutes before. I hadn't realized how much I'd needed a good gulp of oxygen.

I took a few steps to the edge of a small cliff and looked down. We were now quite high up. Birds arced through the air below us. Beyond them was a green valley with a small stream meandering through it. But the area looked damaged, like a war had been fought there. Clumps of trees had been knocked down in a haphazard pattern.

"Hey, are those houses down there?" Fiona pointed to a group of tall pines.

I squinted. Camouflaged by the trees were three long log houses with grass roofs. One was almost completely fallen in. Another was missing its door. Only the house in the middle looked like it would last the whole day. The land in front of the homes was overgrown with brush and weeds.

"They're definitely houses," I said.

Something small dropped to the ground behind us. I turned, but there was nothing there, only a pebble rolling across the path. And yet I had the feeling something, or someone, had just been standing a few feet away.

Fiona was still eyeballing the buildings, shaking her head. "Who built those lovely condos?"

"These could be the ruins from the old settlement. The place doesn't look like it's been lived in for quite awhile."

"Uh oh, I've got some bad news," Fiona said.

"What?"

She pointed to the west. "There's rain coming."

A gray and heavy barrier was moving along the ocean quite a distance away, but I knew it wouldn't be long before it swept across us.

"We better hurry and find a way back," I said. "I don't want to be caught in a downpour. Especially not out here."

We started looking for a path home. The only one we could find led us north, down toward the ruins.

Soon we were out of the rocks and onto grassy soil, thick with nettles and oversized weeds. I was relieved that it was no longer a struggle to find safe footing, but I didn't like the direction we were forced to travel. Thorny brush made an impenetrable wall on either side of us.

"We have to keep going," Fiona said. "I still can't see any easy way to head south. We may have to follow the shore as far as we can."

The vegetation grew heavier and the land boggier as we descended into the valley. My nostrils filled with the stink of fungus. The smell drifted right out of the ground, growing stronger with every footstep. It was too wet here for normal plants to thrive. Only the ones that grew in shade and on the undersides of things took hold. Large green pads of moss had choked out some of the grass. We stepped over the occasional rotted log.

Fiona pointed at an old pine that had been split in two. A small column of smoke still rose from it. A number of other trees nearby had received similar blows. "This place looks like it was shelled by lightning."

I nodded. The hair on my scalp and arms was tingling as if the electric blast had left a residue of energy in the air. "I'd have hated to be standing in the middle of the storm," I said. "Just one bolt would've cut my whole body in two."

"I guess that'd give you a split personality," she joked.

"Oh, ha ha! With quips like that, you're working your way up to being an honorary Icelander."

My words were light-hearted, but I was starting to feel nervous. A vicious storm was on its way, so death by lightning seemed a very real possibility. This got my feet into motion. The valley widened. We crossed a small, sluggish stream using algae-covered rocks as stepping stones. I slipped near the far side and soaked my left shoe.

Fiona grabbed my hand, saying, "I think you need a bit of help with your balance."

I stepped, squished, stepped, squished, next to Fiona, enjoying the feeling of holding her hand. Suddenly the day seemed a lot brighter. I could march on for a thousand miles or so, no problem.

Unfortunately, there was trouble almost right away. We were nearing the ruins. They looked even worse than they had from a distance. Beams broken, doors rotted, mold growing along the windowsills. Vines had crept up the walls and clung onto every corner. Two of the roofs were caved in as if they'd received a blow from a massive fist. I couldn't see any easy way to go around them.

"We'll probably find a path or two on the other side of this place," I said. "When these people were here, whoever they were, they must have made some sort of trails. Maybe they're not completely grown in."

"I hope you're right."

We walked slowly up to the three houses. It'd been at least a hundred years since anyone had lived here. Maybe longer.

Along one of the houses was a shallow pit. In the pit was a large, flat stone with runes written across it, like the ones I'd seen in books on Norse mythology. The stone was cracked in the center and stained with a splotch of red. It looked like someone had only recently dug it up, because fresh dirt was piled over to one side.

I was about to point this out to Fiona when a quick movement at the edge of my vision startled me. Before I could scream, a long arm had reached out and grabbed me by the elbow.

"What are you doing here?" a man grunted.

» 15 «

Fiona gasped. I turned to face my attacker, fists up and ready to fight.

It was my father. His jaw muscles were clenched, his eyes narrowed and he looked about ready to kill me. "What the hell are you doing on this end of the island?"

"I—we—got lost," I stammered, moving a few steps away.

Dad shook his finger. "Do you know how far you've come? I told you to stick close to home."

"We were but we just … uh …"

"We found some pretty cool paths," Fiona finished.

Dad ignored her. He crossed his arms. "Do you know how long I had to argue with your mom to get her to let you come on this trip?"

I clammed up, not sure what to say. I couldn't believe he was flipping out on me in front of Fiona.

"Don't you have anything to say?" Dad asked.

"I'm sorry," I mumbled. "We didn't mean to go this far. We did get lost, honest."

Dad let out his breath. "Where are your bikes?"

"Back there." I motioned over my shoulder. "On the other side of those rocks." I deliberately left out the fact that we'd crawled across the ravine on a tree. And traveled down a bunch of mountain paths.

"Well," Dad said finally, "you're here. There's not much I can do about that now." Was he cooling down? He stared at me, his face unreadable. Then he uncrossed his arms and his look softened. "I was going to show you this place tomorrow anyway."

"Why?" I asked, pretending I hadn't already figured out where we were.

"It's the remains of the settlement I was talking about."

"Really?" I said. "That's cool." I wondered if he could tell I was trying to get on his good side. "How'd you get here, anyway?"

"I rented a boat." He gestured toward a tall, finger-shaped cliff. "It's tied up in a bay over there. This morning I met Harbard and he told me about this place but wasn't interested in ferrying me here. He said I'd already given him enough bad luck to sink seven ships. Then he warned me to be good and gone from this end of the island before dark, because that's when all the spirits from the underworld are loosed and Hel herself walks this valley." Dad shook his head. "I can't tell if he has a really strange sense of humor, or if he's just the most superstitious man in the world."

"Maybe it's a little of both," Fiona offered.

"I hope so. Harbard did mention he might come by this way to make sure I didn't drown. Then he went off, saying he had to work in his garden." Fiona and I exchanged a glance. We'd seen Harbard in his garden, alright. "Any-way, Drang is exactly the place I needed to see. It should really help me figure out the last story in my book. Harbard was kind enough to tell me a little of the island's history. All about the Icelanders who settled here and the hardships they encountered." He paused, then added. "And all the murders that took place."

"Murders? What the heck are you talking about?" Fiona asked. "Uh … I mean, what murders?"

I waved my hands. "No! Don't get Dad talking about anything gory. He won't stop."

"You want to know what happened, just as much as she does," Dad said. I actually didn't, but I figured I was in enough trouble, so I paid attention. "It's an interesting, but strange story. Harbard said fifteen men, nine women and a few children, led by a man named Olavr Tryggvason, came by way of Victoria and landed here in the summer of 1896. They were all Icelanders and they had dreams of forming a new community on Drang. They had no idea how inhospitable this island could be."

"Did the weather drive them away?" Fiona asked.

"No," Dad said, "it was the Mórar ghosts. At least that's what the settlers said. When they first arrived this was a peaceful, warm valley. They knew they didn't have too many months of good weather left, so they quickly built these three longhouses to winter in." Dad led us over to one of the buildings, knocked at the wood wall. "Solid structures, with open hearths in the center to keep everything warm. The fall was rainy and miserable—nothing that would discourage an Icelander. But when the first major winter storm struck them, two of the women froze to death in a matter of hours. It was an unnaturally cold night. The settlers' wood pile was buried under ten inches of ice and their food supply dwindled along with their hope. The ocean was too rough to cross, so they were stuck here. Then the Mórar appeared.

"Apparently the Mórar would first just follow people around after dark, cracking branches and thrusting their ghostly faces in front of travelers. Then they became more aggressive, straddling the rooftops and slamming doors. They were led by an absolutely malevolent specter whom the settlers called Bolverk. They believed he was able to make the dead walk. That's dead animals *and* dead humans. One of the men was apparently attacked by his own dog who had died and been buried the day before. The dog still had dirt caked in his fur. It took three big men with clubs to kill the hound for the second time."

Dad motioned at one of the openings beside us. "Later that night the two women who had frozen to death appeared and probably stood right here, scratching at the doors and windows, begging to be let into the warmth. No one dared open the door. The next morning they found their corpses outside. The settlers said prayers over the women's bodies, then took them out in a boat and dropped them into the wild, rolling ocean.

"But that was just the beginning. Bolverk sent a fetch into one of the settler's dreams. It drove the man so insane, he awoke, grabbed an axe and chopped several of his sleeping fellow settlers to death, then fled. Olavr called together all the men to go into the night and find the murderer, but no one would, so he journeyed out on his own and brought him down."

"Killed him?" I asked.

Dad was rubbing the top of his head, checking out his bald spot. "Probably. At least he was never seen again. When Olavr returned, the others held a vote and decided to leave, even though the ocean was nearly impassable. Olavr stayed on saying his work wasn't finished."

"What work?" Fiona had her arms crossed. I'd never seen her look so serious. She seemed older somehow.

"I don't know. Harbard didn't explain any more than that."

"Well, what about the ghosts?" I asked. "Where did the Icelanders think they were from? Were they Indian ghosts?"

"Exactly! What about the ghosts!" Dad pointed one finger in the air and waved it around to add emphasis to his words. "I had the same question. I found a couple things here that shed a lot of light on the story of the settlement. And maybe why it went so wrong. If you believe in bad luck, that is. Come here." He led us around the corner of the ruin. A part of the wall had collapsed and the earth had sunk down, almost like an underground chamber had fallen in. "I was snooping around here, just soaking up the atmosphere. And I found this." Dad knelt and pushed some of the dirt away from the side and revealed a line of disintegrated timbers below the longhouse. "This building was constructed on top of an older one. The settlers probably didn't even know it was there. Now, it's pretty strange that there was another house here. I know the Natives didn't make homes like this. But there's more."

Dad led us back to the stone we'd been looking at a few minutes before. He adjusted his glasses, squinted down. "That rock has probably been here longer than the settlers' longhouses."

"Why does it have red marks on it?" I asked.

"Uh … I'm not sure," Dad said. "The runes are the most interesting thing about it. I'm a little rusty at reading them, and many aren't familiar to me, but it looks like they're part of a prophecy. Or some kind of chant about the end of the world. It says: *An axe age, a sword age, shields will be bashed, then a wolf age, a fang age, and brothers will be drenched in the blood of brothers. Take this sacrifice, Father of wolves, Sire of snakes.*

Unleash your son, Jormungand. A new world will rise from the venom and fire."

Dad's last words echoed around us. "But people haven't written with runes for hundreds and hundreds of years," I said. "Did the Icelandic settlers make this stone?"

"No," Dad answered. "It wasn't them. If my guess is right, Vikings built the older structure and carved the runes almost a thousand years ago. And those Vikings were called the Mórar."

"The ghosts settled this place?" Fiona was looking about as confused as I felt. "What do you mean?"

Dad gave her an almost wicked grin. He got a big charge out of reeling people into his stories. It was probably a genetic thing, passed down through generations of storytelling Icelanders. "They called them the Mórar, which means ghost. There were always lots of names for spirits depending on which part of Iceland you were from: fetches, *afturganga, skottur, draugr.* The more names you knew, the better. There was power in naming things. Sometimes that would be enough to dispel them.

"So Mórar was just another name for ghosts. But it's *also* the name of a group of Icelanders who, about a thousand years ago, were banished from northern Iceland near Reykir. In fact they were from the same area our family came from. It might even have been our ancestors who drove them out of Iceland. Kind of neat, eh? We drive them away, then a thousand years later we find their resting place."

Actually it didn't sound neat to me. I found it a little unnerving.

Dad leaned against the longhouse. "The Mórar were the worst of the worst, accused of sorcery and unholy sacrifice and said to be closer kin to wolves than men. They worshipped Loki and his two giant sons, Jormungand and Fenrir. The Mórar's leader was a sorcerer named Bolverk." Dad paused. "Bolverk is another one of those names from the old days. Odin used it whenever he was going to do something bad."

"You mean Odin was a bad guy?" Fiona asked.

"He was both good and evil, full of pride and greed just like many people are. The Vikings believed Odin was the highest of the gods, but most Norsemen worshipped Thor. They liked him because he was a tough, strong, honest god. Simple and straightforward. This meant a lot of tricks got played on him, but he was still the one all the gods turned to when they needed some extra muscle. But as much as the Icelanders identified with Thor, they never forgot to pay their respects to Odin, the one-eyed Allfather.

"Anyway, the name Bolverk means 'worker of evil.' And if the legends are even partly true, this sorcerer lived up to his name a hundred times over. Drinking the blood of snakes to prolong his life, sacrificing horses that had been run until they were slick with sweat, and other macabre stuff like that. The people of northern Iceland chased the Mórar away before they grew too strong.

"They fled across the North Sea and eventually made their way into what's now Russia. They plundered for a time, until their ships were sunk by Byzantine soldiers and they were forced onto the land. No one heard of them again, though there are legends that a few of them survived and were able to make it to the east coast of Russia and build a longship. From there they might have struck out to find a new home. And landed here."

"They came all the way from Russia?" I asked. "Isn't that a little far?"

"It's not entirely impossible. The Vikings expanded as far west as Newfoundland, as far south as Sicily and Greece and as far east as the Ural Mountains of Russia. They were amazing navigators and loved the ocean unlike any other race. The Mórar were among the hardiest of them all. But if they landed here they were likely only a few in number, with no resources. One bad winter would have meant the end of their food supply and of them. Or they may have died of sickness."

Dad fell silent. The clouds had shifted across half the sky, blotting out the sun. A cool breeze was snaking its way through the valley. I shivered.

"Come this way." Dad led us into the one longhouse that still had its roof intact. We stopped a few feet inside the door. Gray light filtered through cracks in the wall, revealing a cobwebbed interior and a dirt floor. Another door, half disintegrated, was open at the far end. Two walls, which used to separate different parts of the building, were now collapsed.

"There … it's a bit warmer in here," Dad said, then carried on like a teacher who'd been interrupted half way through a lesson. "Whether the Mórar were here or not is a moot point. It'd take a team of archeologists to prove that. But the Icelandic settlers believed the Mórar ghosts were here. And that was enough to make them leave. I have no idea why Olavr chose to stay." Dad paused. "He was quite the man though. He lived on Drang until his death in 1947." Then Dad turned to me and said, "You've already met his son."

"I have?"

"Yeah. Harbard. Olavr married at an old age. Longevity was one of his family's traits."

I found it hard to imagine Harbard having a father. Had he been just as grumpy as Harbard? Thinking of his dead father reminded me of the cairns. "Did Harbard men-

tion the burial mounds?"

"Mounds? Where?" Dad asked.

I told him. Then decided I should tell him about the dead goat, too. He listened intently. "The cairns must be quite old," he said when I was finished. "The settlers wouldn't have built them; they buried their dead in the sea because they feared their bodies would fall under the control of the Mórar. And I don't think the Natives would've built mounds like that. I have no idea what the goat thing is all about. No idea at all. It does make me wonder about the runes on that stone out there and why it's been stained red, almost like it was part of some ceremony. Sure am curious about who dug up the stone in the first place." He paused and I saw the worry on his face. He glanced at his watch. "It's almost supper time. We should head for home." Then he looked at Fiona. "Were your parents expecting you to be away this long?"

"Well …" Fiona started. She cleared her throat. "To tell you the truth, they actually don't know I'm even here."

It took a moment for the words to register with Dad. "What do you mean?"

"We had a misunderstanding. I kinda slipped away from home and came to Drang on my own."

"You've been here for almost two whole days? Won't they be sick with worry?"

Fiona couldn't meet his eyes. She looked at the ground, her jaw muscles clenched. "Yeah, probably by now. I guess I was too mad to really care." She fell silent.

No one said anything for a few uncomfortable moments. But I heard something. A familiar sound was beginning to register in my brain.

Footsteps. Outside. Soft, determined footsteps.

"Close the doors," I whispered.

"What?" said Fiona.

"Close the doors!" I yelled. I ran to the front of the house. A light, misty rain had just begun turning everything outside to silver. I yanked on the door, but it wouldn't budge.

"Michael! Have you gone off your rocker?" Dad was a step behind me. "What are you doing?"

Then a wolf's howl cut through the air. Just a few feet away.

It was a long, mournful wail, reverberating through the air, drawing some secret hidden panic and fear from deep inside me.

"A wolf?" Fiona whispered, her voice shaky. "But there aren't any wolves on Drang Island."

» 17 «

We stood, paralyzed by the sound.

A second wolf answered the howl, their voices overlapping.

"They're right outside!" Dad stepped past me, grabbed hold of the door and yanked it shut. Part of it came away in his hands. "Quick, close the other door!"

Fiona was the first there, tugging at the door. I dashed across the room, joined her, pulling until the door was shut as tight as possible. The wood was flimsy. I found a long piece of half-rotted timber and lodged it across as a brace.

We gathered in the center of the room. I picked up a stone that had fallen from the hearth. Fiona dug in her pocket and pulled out a jackknife. She opened the blade. It was about three inches long.

"If we just stay still," Dad whispered, "they might go away."

None of us moved. We breathed in and out as one.

There was growling. Then a gruff word was spoken by a man and the wolves fell silent. I strained my ears, but all I heard was the wind whistling through cracks in the house. A pitter patter of soft raindrops on the roof. Water dripped down onto the floor.

There was a two-inch-wide hole a few feet away from me that looked out to the front of the longhouse. I crept up to it and put my eye to the opening. Outside it was dull, misty. Lightning flashed in the distance, backlighting the trees.

Then something moved, covering the hole. I was suddenly looking into a large human eye sunk into a pale mottled face, the color leached from the iris, the pupils black. An eye that blazed with anger and power.

The stone I'd been carrying slipped out of my fingers. I couldn't back away or cry out: the eye held me in place, silenced me. Strength drained from my body straight into that glowing orb. Never to return. Even my heartbeat slowed, the blood in my veins seemed sluggish.

Something huge exhaled on the other side of the wall, its breath a thick, ice-cold vapor wafting in through the cracks, chilling my skin. A scent of sweet decay followed, as if it had been eating flowers. The shape leaned closer against the wall. A low creaking sound came from inside the wood, the timber was bending slowly. The eye neared. Grew larger.

"Chose you," an eerie voice rasped, *"I chose all three of you."*

I tried to open my mouth, but it was frozen shut. A new break appeared in the wall, directly across from my throat. White, thin fingers wiggled, slowly reaching in, quietly pushing aside the rotted wood.

"What do you see?" Dad asked. His voice came from a great distance, almost another world. "Is there anything out there?"

I sucked the slightest bit of air into my lungs, tried to force it back out in the form of a word. Failed.

"Michael?" Fiona asked. "What's wrong?" Her questions echoed around me.

The hand was getting closer. Grasping at the open air,

fingers brushing my Adam's apple.

"Michael," Fiona's voice floated nearby. "Are—"

The hand grabbed hold of my neck, yanked me against the wall, trying to pull me through the wood. I found some last bit of strength and pushed back, struggling against it as the fingers tightened around my windpipe, cutting off my air. Fiona yelled something, clutched my shoulder and heaved. Dad did, too. Still, we weren't strong enough.

The man on the other side began to laugh, a deep rumbling guffaw that shook the longhouse.

Then metal flashed, the laughter was cut short and I was free. I fell back, gasping for air. I glimpsed a white, long-fingered hand with the jackknife embedded in its wrist. There was no blood. The hand was yanked back through the hole.

Dad drew us away from the wall.

"Who's out there?" Fiona gasped. Her eyes were wide and wild.

"Stay calm," Dad commanded, his voice cracking. "We've got to stay calm. What'd you see, Michael?"

I rubbed my throat. "J-just an eye. And then a hand. I couldn't tell who or what it was."

"Well, I guess we've got more than wolves to worry about," Dad said, sounding desperate. He barked orders like a general. "Grab a piece of wood or a rock. Keep your eyes open, tell me if you spot anything. We can only hope we've scared him off."

I didn't think so. Not after looking into that pool of anger. And why didn't he cry out when he was stabbed? Didn't it hurt? And if that didn't hurt, then what would?

I found a long stick, thick enough to deliver a substantial blow. Fiona had picked up a similar weapon. We gathered in the center of the house again, keeping as far away from the walls as possible.

"We might have to make a run for it," Dad said. "If it's just a man, maybe we have a chance. I haven't heard the wolves for awhile; whoever it was must have scared them away."

"Where do we go?" I asked.

"Toward the boat," he answered. "I'll lead the way."

"But—" Fiona started.

A booming crash cut off her question. Something had landed on the roof and was stomping around up there, pounding on the wood. The timbers shook, splinters and sod rained down. The noises ended suddenly.

Then came a thud as if a heavy weight had hit the ground. The door at the front rattled so hard it nearly fell off. Then the shaking stopped.

"He's playing with us," Dad said, softly. "It's just a game for him."

Our attacker started pounding on the walls, chunks of wood flew across the open area, one of the boards snapped in two and I glimpsed a shifting figure. Then silence.

But not complete silence. Now there was the sniffling of an animal and a low growl reverberated through the interior of the longhouse. Finally, a word, whispered so deep it was really little more than a rumble: *"Ormr."*

Dad sucked in his breath. The word had some meaning to him, but he didn't share it. "We have to get out," he whispered.

Something began moving along the floor at the front of the house. A long thin apparition. It appeared in the light, then disappeared. Followed by another and another, coming out of holes in the ground. Ebony-skinned shapes that slithered across the floor toward us.

I heard a rattle, like a baby's toy. Shaking back and forth.

"Snakes," I whispered.

A second rattle shook. A third. Serpents were advancing in waves.

"Get out!" Dad yelled. "Out the back!"

We ran. I was first to the door, pulling off the piece of wood that I'd put there to block it. A dark shape shot from a nearby ledge, latched onto my right wrist. Pain burst in my flesh, burned all the way up my arm. I looked down to see the green glowing eyes of a serpent staring into mine.

» 18 «

Its fangs were sunk deep into my wrist and it was trying to wrap its ink-black body around my arm.

I screamed. Shook my arm until the snake flew off and landed on the far side of the hut.

Then Dad pushed me into the open.

We ran blindly, out behind the longhouse and up a small embankment made treacherous by the soft rain. Dad led us higher, through bushes, our feet pounding madly in the earth. I grabbed at branches, using them to pull myself up. I looked back. No one seemed to be following us.

We didn't dare slow down. My arm ached with a numb pain that was spreading from joint to joint. Hadn't Fiona said something about staying still if you got a snake bite? How movement would hurry the poison through your veins?

We charged on. Dad was only a few steps ahead, breaking the path, but I had to struggle to keep up. His legs were so long I started to lose ground. We cut through a series of low-hanging trees. I covered my face with my arms and crashed through them into the open.

A dark figure was right in my path, arms stretched out and its mouth wide. It was one of those creatures we'd seen before, but this one was even larger than the last. It hissed, loudly. I fell to one side, trying to avoid touching the beast, rolled over and looked up to see that it had vanished yet again. I was alone. Dad had run ahead without me.

Fiona cried out from a long distance away. I'd lost track of her and somehow she'd lagged behind. She yelled again, her voice echoing, making it hard to tell where it was coming from. She sounded like she was in pain.

I spotted a flash of her red hair in the mist. "Dad!" I shouted, hoping he would somehow hear me. "We've lost Fiona. She's still back there!"

I ran toward her, over rough land, past dead pine trees. I found her on the ground, pulling at her foot. It had been jammed between a rock and a twisted, thick, tree root. "Help me!" she yelled.

I bent down, started yanking on her leg until she let out a cry of pain. "You're gonna break my ankle!"

"Can we undo your boot?" I asked, quickly looking around for signs of danger.

"I tried. The laces are double-knotted. They're too slippery to get a grip on."

"Then hold on. We have to do this the hard way." I grabbed onto her shoulders and tugged, digging in with my feet. She grunted, pushing with her other leg. Finally, her foot broke free and we landed in a heap. I scrambled to my feet and helped her up. "Can you walk?"

She nodded and looked around. "I nearly tripped over one of those stupid little creatures. Then suddenly I was caught in this root. The thing laughed at me, then went running back toward the cabin."

"I saw one, too," I said. "They seem to be all over the place."

Rain was now tapping heavily against the leaves. The

drops were getting bigger. Branches snapped in the distance.

"Where's your father?" Fiona asked.

"He mustn't have heard me call to him. He's probably up ahead, looking for us."

We hurried back across fallen trees and up to the top of the valley to where I'd last seen Dad. There was no sign of him.

"I think this is the way to the boat. He must have gone there," I whispered. "I hope that's where he went."

"Should we keep going?"

I looked back. There were rows upon rows of trees, fog twisting through them. He could be anywhere. "I don't know," I admitted.

Then I heard a shifting sound, a shuffling in the mist that rolled toward us, growing thicker. A shadow lumbered forward through the haze: a man-like shape. Dead trees fell and live ones shook as each step sent a shock wave through the ground.

A voice reached us, a strange eerie singing.

Hullabulla lullabulla
bones and red blood
in a dark flood.

Each step he took made the pain in my arm double. Every note in his song mesmerized me. I felt drawn toward his presence. An ever-widening circle of power, getting nearer and nearer.

Hullabulla lullabulla
heart in red blood
in a dark flood.

Fiona was standing as still as a deer caught in a car's headlights.

Then from another direction came a different man,

dressed in rags, shambling out of the mist, waving his arms. His skin white and dead-looking. His mouth moving wildly, guttural words pouring out. *"Go wan get out ov ere! Un! Un!"*

"Run!" Fiona yelled.

The urgency in her voice broke the spell. I ran with her along the path, scrambling through the trees. We dashed wildly down a low hill. All the while a ghostly voice called from behind, laughing, whooping and mocking us as we fled, making me feel that every motion was futile. We'd never get away.

We burst out of the trees into a large bay, sliding the final few feet down an escarpment. We skidded to a halt among sharp piles of scree. "There's the boat," Fiona yelled. It was a small one sitting lopsided and lying partly out of the water. It had an outboard motor.

We dashed along the thin line of sand for about fifty yards, forced to splash through a few inches of water. My father wasn't anywhere to be seen. "Start it!" Fiona yelled as we climbed into the boat. "Start it!"

"But we can't leave Dad!"

"Just get out into the water!" She pointed behind me. Two wolves, one gray and one black, were loping across the beach toward us.

The boat was too far onto the sand to go anywhere. I jumped down and pushed it into the bay until I was up to my hips; then I climbed aboard. The second I was in, Fiona yanked back on the pull start. The motor sputtered. She tried it again. The wolves were nearing, splashing through the water in their mad dash toward us, tongues hanging out between their jaws. Their eyes glowed red.

The waves drove us back toward the shore.

"Again! Try again!" I yelled.

Fiona flicked a switch, pressed a button. Then gave it another desperate pull.

The motor fired and she hit the gas. I fell back and we plowed a few feet into the water.

But it wasn't far enough. The black wolf leapt and landed half way inside the boat. It dug in with its back legs, threatening to capsize us. It snapped its jaws. Some of the fur was missing from its head, revealing white skull beneath. One of its front paws had no flesh at all, just claws and bones.

I grabbed an oar and whacked the beast, but this only seemed to enrage it. The wolf now had its hind leg hooked on the edge, was about to climb in. I smacked it again. At the same moment Fiona cranked on the tiller, launching the wolf into the sea. It disappeared under the waves.

Then we were away. Farther and farther, out into the deep part of the bay. We circled around. The waves were growing higher. Wind pasted my hair to the side of my head. "Stay close, Fiona. Dad may show up." We looked back. The wolf had crawled out of the water and joined its companion on the shore, waiting for us.

I found two life jackets under the seat and we quickly pulled them on.

"We can't stay out here forever. We'll run out of gas," Fiona said.

"We've got to get help. We'll have to go back to the campground. Let's head this way," I said and pointed west.

Fiona gunned the motor and we started out of the bay. I looked back. The wolves were still there, eyes glowing, teeth bared, but I saw no sign of the ghoulish men. Or of Dad.

We roared out of the bay, the cliffs sloped up before us.

On the edge of a precipice stood a tall man, wind stirring his garments and small black shadows dancing around him. He was holding onto another man by the scruff of the neck. I recognized Dad's shirt. His head was hanging down. Was the man going to throw Dad from the cliff?

I yelled at Fiona to look up.

The man gestured with a staff, out at the ocean.

In the distance the sky looked clearer. There was another boat coming our way. Maybe they had a radio or could help us. Just as I stretched out my arms to wave them down, a giant shape rose up in the open water.

We struck it with the force of a battering ram.

The boat disintegrated under us.

» 19 «

By all rights I should've been slammed to pieces against the shore. Or drowned and dragged down to the depths.

Instead, I bobbed to the surface and drifted. Salt water stung my eyes and the scrapes on my body. I don't remember even trying to swim. All I recall is staring at the darkening sky and listening to the water swishing all around me. But I was moving. Not back and forth with the waves, but ahead. Like I was being pushed by a single, determined wave. Carried onwards and away.

At times I thought I could hear Fiona moaning.

Then a dark hull appeared; a motor revved down. Two hands clamped onto my shirt and I was dragged from the water, lifted by strong arms and dropped down onto a wooden deck like a landed fish. A harsh voice spit out words that exploded around me. There was a pause in this barrage as another catch was hauled in and dropped next to me.

I opened my eyes to a grisly beard and sky blue eyes glowering down at me.

Harbard.

"You're alive," he said, sounding disappointed. "You looked like you'd become a shade. What were you doing in the water with a storm about to start?"

I couldn't answer. My tongue was trapped in my mouth, feeling swollen by salt.

From beside me came a moan, then coughing. Fiona was lying there, stirring as if in a fitful sleep. A cut on her forehead bled freely.

Harbard leaned closer. His teeth were stained yellow. "I saw you on the hill above my home. You and your friend. Taunting me. Bad luck comes from bad doings."

He was getting too close. I tried to push him away, but all I could do was lift my right arm a little and drop it to my side again. At least this attracted his attention to the snake bite. His eyes opened wide in surprise. "You've been bitten!" He grabbed my wrist, pulled it toward him like he'd forgotten I was attached to it. He prodded at the wound, sending a bolt of pain down my arm. *"Draumur snákur,"* he mumbled. The words gave me a chill. "Where did you get this bite?" Harbard was squeezing my arm now. "Tell me!"

I opened my mouth, but only a hiss of air came out. My vocal chords seemed to have dissolved. Harbard pulled a flask from his jacket, twisted off the cap. Before I could move he latched onto the back of my head, yanked me up and dumped a burning liquid into my mouth. The concoction blazed a trail down my throat and into my stomach. I sat up, leaned over and coughed for a painful minute. Finally, I spat over the side of the boat.

"Answer me," he commanded. "Where did you get this bite?" Then a sudden look of genuine fear came over him and he said with more urgency, "Where is your father?"

"Back there," I pointed. I'd finally found my tongue. "He's back there. Not safe." Harbard kept asking me more questions, but I found it hard to put everything that happened into words. I did my best. When I mentioned the burial mounds, his look of concern turned to horror.

"One was broken open? Then my father's work is undone. And the afturganga is loose."

"Who?" I coughed.

He handed the metal flask to me. "Drink this. Be still, or you'll make the venom spread."

"What! Am I poisoned?"

"No. Only your mind will be poisoned. Sit there and don't move." He pointed at the far end of the ferry. I pulled myself backwards and could barely find the strength to lean against the side of the boat. Only my mind would be poisoned? What could that mean?

Fiona lifted her head, looked at me. "I have a splitting headache," she announced. Then she closed her eyes. The cut on her forehead had stopped bleeding. I reached out to touch her shoulder and try to wake her up.

Harbard gunned the motor, knocking me back, cracking my skull against the bench. Now I was really awake.

"Where are we going?" I shouted.

"To the dock. I'm taking you back."

"But what about Dad? He needs help right now!" I struggled to get up. My legs folded under me like a newborn colt's and I slammed into the deck.

"Stay still!" Harbard scolded. "I'll try to find your father. You two are of no use to anyone now."

I didn't have the energy to argue with him. Harbard urged every last ounce of speed out of the ferry, sending us crashing over waves, charging toward our destination.

I pulled myself closer to Fiona, leaned against her, but decided to let her sleep. I softly pushed an old fishnet beneath her head, hoping that would give her some comfort. Then I examined my arm. There were two holes just past my wrist, oozing blood. The wound tingled and that part of my arm felt deadened. The tingling seemed to be spreading through my body.

I couldn't stop thinking about my father and the man on the cliff holding him by the neck. The image sickened me and at the same time angered me. What did that bushman —or whatever he was—want with him? With any of us?

He'd said, *"I chose you. I chose all three of you."* Which made me think he had something to do with the graffiti on our tent, that he could have been following us from the moment we set foot on this island.

After what seemed hours, Harbard turned into the bay that led to the campground. I pulled myself up enough to see out of the boat. We charged at the dock so fast I thought we'd collide with it. Then Harbard reversed the motor and we banged into place next to a post. I fell over. He limped up to me, grabbed my good arm.

"You'll get out here," he explained. He lifted me and dropped me onto the dock. Air whooshed out of my lungs. A moment later I heard Fiona shout, "Hey, what are you doing?"

Harbard groaned from exertion. Fiona landed beside me. "Ow!" she cried.

Harbard tossed the flask onto my chest. "Drink the rest of this. When they come for you, tell them to wrap you in blankets. And to feed both of you garlic."

Then before I could move, he was gone, the ferry plowing out into the bay. I stood slowly.

"What was that old turd doing with us?" Fiona asked. She was sitting up now, holding the side of her head. "And why are you so pale?"

I showed her my snake bite. She studied it carefully. "It's a clean wound, no swelling. Did you see what kind of snake it was?"

"It was black, that's all I know."

"Good." She sounded relieved. "It wasn't a Pacific rattler then. They aren't black. And they're the only poisonous thing in these parts."

"Harbard knew what it was. He called it by a weird name. 'Dramer snaker' or something like that."

Fiona frowned. "That could mean anything."

I nodded. "It's probably an Icelandic name. Though it does sound a little like 'dream snake,' doesn't it?"

"Whatever it is, you should probably put some antiseptic on it."

I held my arm up against my chest. "What about you? That's a nasty cut on your head?"

"Yeah. It feels like someone was playing hockey inside my skull." She gently touched the wound. "I think the boat must have hit one big rock. But it seemed like it rose right out of the water on its own."

I swallowed. "What if it wasn't a rock?"

"What do you mean?"

"Well you said it looked like it rose out of the water on its own. What if something did?"

"Like a whale?"

"No, some kind of sea serpent. I know it sounds nuts, but we've seen it twice now, just the back of it. There's even a place where people sacrifice goats to it. Maybe it really exists. Maybe Harbard's not as crazy as we think he is."

"You can't be right," she said softly. "You can't be."

We were silent for a while. This was almost too big to comprehend. I offered Harbard's flask to Fiona, but she took one whiff and handed it back. I drained it. The substance returned life to my limbs. "We need to get help. We're gonna have to find the ranger," I said.

"He's probably already looking for me. My parents would have called him by now."

"Does that mean you want to stay here?"

She shook her head. "No. I guess it's time to talk to Mom and Dad. This isn't exactly a normal trip away from home anymore. Besides, it'll take both of us to convince the ranger that there's something really bizarre going on here."

A few minutes later we were in the center of the campground, looking at the front of an old, square, tin-roofed building. The words PARK RANGER were stenciled on the door. The wind and rain had faded the words and cracks were creeping through the wood.

Fiona went in first, saying, "Whatever you do, don't mention sea serpents." The floors were hardwood and there was a long counter that ran from one wall to the other. It looked like a bar, except there were no bottles or glasses hanging from the roof. Maps were pinned to the wall beside a bulletin board with a big sign that said, "DON'T FORGET THE LONG WEEKEND RUSH!"

There was no one around.

I stepped up to the counter, found a bell and rang it. The *ding* sound echoed around us. We waited.

Ding.

A door opened behind the counter and out came Ranger Morrison. He was smiling until he saw us. Then his face became grumpy. He bellied up to the counter. "What do you two want?"

"We have to report a missing person," I said.

The surprise showed on the ranger's face. "A missing person?"

"Yes, my dad has been captured."

Morrison looked from me to Fiona. "Is this some kind of stupid joke?"

I shook my head. I felt numb.

"Who did it?" he asked. "And where?"

I repeated the story, speaking slowly, awkwardly at first, explaining our bike trip, meeting up with Dad, and about the one man who hounded us at the longhouse and the other who later came out of the woods, waving his arms. Ranger Morrison eyed me with contempt and seemed to be biting his tongue, but his face turned pale when I mentioned Harbard.

"Harbard's looking for him?" Morrison asked. I was glad there was at least one person on this island he respected. "This sounds too much like that Siroiska thing all over again, mystery upon mystery. And almost a year to the day since he disappeared. You two sit down." He gestured at some chairs set by the wall. Fiona and I sat. Morrison grabbed a medical package from behind the counter, trudged over and handed it to Fiona. Then he disappeared into the back, came out a minute later with two cups of tea. The bags were still floating in the steaming water.

He looked down. "What's your name again?"

"Michael Asmundson."

He gestured at Fiona. "And you?"

She straightened. "Fiona."

"Fiona who?"

"Fiona Gavin." She sounded almost proud when she said this.

"Where are your parents?"

This was it, I thought. She was going to be in trouble.

"Gone," she answered after a short pause. "To Seattle. On business. I'm on holidays with Michael and his dad."

The lie came pretty easily to Fiona. Like she'd been practicing it all day. I wasn't sure if this was a good time to lie or not.

Morrison stared at her, then at me. "I think you two made half this stuff up," he said heavily. "But my instincts tell me to believe the other half. Now I just gotta figure out what to do." He took a couple of steps away, then said to me, "The funny thing is, I was looking for you and your dad at about eleven this morning."

"Why?"

"Because your sister called here. It sounded kind of urgent, though she wouldn't tell me what it was." He pointed at a pay phone on the wall. "You can use that if you want. I'll be busy for a few minutes." He went into his office.

Fiona grabbed a plastic spoon from the table, removed her tea bag and had a sip. Then she dug in the medic kit, found an antiseptic and poured some on my bite.

"Ouch!" I cried. "Aren't you supposed to warn me first?"

"It wouldn't be half as much fun." She patted it gently with a cotton ball. It seemed like the wound was shrinking already. She stuck a bandage to my skin. "I had to lie to him," she whispered.

"Why?"

"Because if he knew I'd run away, he wouldn't have believed our story. He obviously doesn't know anything about me; maybe he hasn't checked his messages or something. I'll phone my parents when we're done here." Fiona felt her forehead. "How's my cut look?"

"The blood's all dry. It's really not much more than a scratch," I answered.

"Too bad. I was hoping to get a cool scar." She smiled at me, then poked through the medic kit, examining its contents.

"Is there garlic in there?" I asked.

"Garlic?"

"Yeah, Harbard said we should eat garlic."

Fiona shrugged. "I doubt there's garlic anywhere on this island. He's probably being superstitious. Maybe he eats it all the time." She paused. "That would explain why he doesn't have too many friends."

I grinned. Then I shivered. My body still seemed out of whack. I sipped the tea. It did warm me up, if only for a few minutes.

I knew I should phone home to at least tell them what was going on. And to find out why Sarah was calling.

"Your dad's gonna be alright," Fiona whispered. And then she started saying something else, but her words faded out. My arm grew numb. A part of me receded from everything. I closed my eyes, then opened them again.

All the color had drained from the room. Everything was painted in gray tones. Something moved in the corner of my vision and I tried to look directly at it, but it stayed just out of sight. For a second I thought I'd seen a black, human shape. Watching us. A leering smile on its ebony face.

"Michael," it hissed.

» 21 «

The thing started to move closer, coming fully into my vision, reaching toward me with long, spidery fingers.

"Michael. Michael."

I blinked. The room swirled back into full color.

"Michael." Fiona tapped gently on my head. "Michael, are you there? Hello!"

It took me a moment to register what she'd just said. I looked around, but the dark form had vanished.

"Sorry, I just kinda spaced out there," I explained. "I'm gonna walk a bit." I stood, then meandered slowly around the room, trying to get my bearings while Fiona watched me. I spotted a small clock and was surprised to see it was 7:15 at night. I went to the phone and dialed home collect.

"Are you alright?" Sarah asked before I could even say hello.

"Y-yes, of course."

"Are you sure?" She sounded like she didn't believe me. "I had this awful feeling just moments ago that you were in danger. Like something bad was—I don't know—glaring at you. Waiting for the right time to strike. Is everything okay?"

I looked around the room. Blinked. I still couldn't see any more strange shapes. "Yes, I think we're safe. We're in a police—that is—a ranger's office. Uh … is Mom home?"

"No, she went to town. What's going on, Michael?"

I told her about Dad—about everything—as quickly as I could.

"I see," she said, slowly. She didn't sound surprised at all or else she was really good at hiding it. "Now some things are making sense."

"What things?"

"I had a dream last night. About the island you guys are on. It was … it was a saga dream, Michael. Like Grandpa talked about, a dream that is more than a dream. I saw you with a stone in your hand. You said something about using it to shake the roots of the world tree. And there was this storm full of Valkyries and warriors, all charging across the sky to battle."

If there was anything I'd learned in my life, it was to trust Sarah when she said she'd had a dream. She once told me to stay home from a school trip, so I did, pretending I was sick. One of my classmates accidentally had his arm broken in several places at a metal factory. I always wondered if it was supposed to have been me.

"Do you have any idea what the dream meant?" I asked.

Sarah was silent for a moment. "It had Yggdrasill in it. The world tree."

"Yes, I know what Yggdrasill is." We were always competing with each other to see who knew more about the old Norse myths.

"Something more is going to happen there at Drang. Something big. And it has to do with life and death, because Yggdrasill is the tree that goes from life to death." She paused. "Look, just get off the island. It isn't safe there."

"You're overreacting, Sarah," I said. "Everything's going to be okay." But part of me agreed with her. We should leave and let the ranger and the police handle everything. But what about Dad?

"Just don't do anything … I don't know … brave or stupid. Swear on Grandma Gunnora's grave," she whispered. In our family this was the strongest oath we could make.

"I swear."

Ranger Morrison came out of the back room. He started talking to Fiona.

"I should go," I said.

"Take care of yourself, Michael. Okay?"

"I will." I hung up.

"Are you ready?" Ranger Morrison asked me.

"Ready for what?"

"To show me where to look for your father."

"What he's saying," Fiona explained, "is he doesn't trust us."

» 22 «

"Listen kid!" Ranger Morrison snarled. "I'll make up my own mind about this so-called sacrificial place. I need to see it with my own two eyes, then, if necessary, I'll radio for help from there. The Mounties don't appreciate being called in for nothing."

"You're risking my father's life by delaying," I said.

He glared down at me, then spoke slowly and clearly. "I do things by the book. Now let's get going while we still have a few hours of light." He headed toward the door. I exchanged a glance with Fiona, who still looked boiling mad. I knew we only had one choice.

"We have to go," I whispered. "What about your parents?"

"I'll phone them when we get back."

We followed Ranger Morrison down to the dock and climbed into his boat, which was slightly larger than Harbard's. After putting on our life jackets, we headed out to sea. A line of clouds cloaked the top of the sky, gathering like unraveling spools of dark wool that shrouded the north end of the island.

The next few minutes drifted by. I stared at the rock walls of Drang as they blurred past, waves crashing relentlessly against the gray stone. I saw a small bay with a dock and a series of stairs that climbed up a low cliff. I assumed that was where Harbard lived.

The boat roared on, battling the water. The clouds above us were growing heavier.

"Do you know who would kidnap his dad?" Fiona asked the ranger.

Morrison furrowed his brow. His jaw was set and I wasn't sure if he was going to speak. "I don't," he finally admitted. "Maybe someone who lives in the bush. I often get reports from fishermen who see smoke on the north end of the island. What did Harbard tell you?"

"He spoke about his dad," I said, "when I told him the burial cairns were broken open. He said something like 'My father's work is undone' and that 'something was let loose.'"

Morrison cocked his head to one side. "I haven't a clue what that means. I came here long after his father was dead. People say he was just as strange as Harbard."

The ocean was growing harsher and my stomach answered with a familiar queasiness. I looked back toward the land as we rounded a corner. I spotted the slide made of stone. "We're here," I shouted. "This is it."

Morrison pulled down on the throttle and cut the engine to quarter speed. We floated to the base of the slide. It took him a few moments to moor the boat to an outcropping. "I'll go up first. You two follow when I pass the rope." For someone who was overweight, he climbed the slide with surprising ease.

He stood at the top. "It smells like a slaughterhouse," he yelled. Then he attached the rope to a small tree and lowered it down.

I headed up the slide, digging in with my feet. Fiona was one step behind. When I got to the top, Ranger Morrison was staring at the ravine. His face was ashen. "Maybe there really is something going on."

The bones were still there. So was the stake and a freshly killed goat.

A thin trail of blood led from the goat to the slide.

"You did say there were two men, right?" Morrison asked.

"Yes," Fiona answered. "One came out of the woods at us. Shouting."

Morrison pointed at the steel pole. "Do you have any idea what these guys hoped to accomplish with this ... this sacrifice?"

I looked at the symbol of Jormungand. "I can't believe I'm saying this, but I think they were going to summon something."

"Like a seance?" the ranger asked.

"No, a special ceremony to bring something up that slide. A sea monster."

Morrison shook his head. "That doesn't make any sense. Who'd be dumb enough to believe in sea monsters?"

Me, I thought. "Someone does," I said. "That's why they built this place."

Morrison stepped closer to the stake. We followed, carefully finding our footing on the steep slope. The closer we got to the goat, the harder it became to inhale. It was like the air was thicker here, the gravity stronger. A few pellets of rain landed, stirring up the smell of the dead animal.

The moment I got near the steel pole, the bite on my

arm flared up with a burning pain and my heart stopped beating. I wobbled for a second.

"Michael, what's wrong?" Fiona asked. She grabbed my shoulder.

"*Harrrrrt,*" I moaned. The blood was frozen in my veins. What was wrong with my heart?

I opened my eyes. The world had drained of all colors but two—I was seeing everything in black and white. Shadowy shapes were flitting around us, darting here and there, pointing and laughing. Two of them pulled on Morrison's pant legs, but he didn't notice. A dark silhouette slipped right in front of my face, its mouth a huge smile. It stuck its hand in the middle of my chest and I felt a sharp pain.

THUD-THUD-THUD-THUD.

I pulled back. Blinked again.

My heart was beating. Air filled my lungs. The real world returned.

Both Morrison and Fiona were staring at me. "Sorry," I whispered, "I felt queasy for a s-second. I just need to sit down." Fiona took me to a large, flat-topped stone. I sat. I was still wheezing, so I took off my life jacket and let it fall behind me. Fiona settled in next to me, put one arm around my shoulder.

"I had some kind of hallucination," I admitted. "And I had one back at the office, too. I think it's the snake bite. Harbard said it would affect my mind."

"What did you see?"

"Black shapes. Dancing around us."

"I did too, just a moment ago," Fiona whispered. "They looked like the creature that followed us today. Then they vanished."

We were silent for a moment. "What if they're real?" I asked.

"What?"

"I just … I wonder why we both saw them? It's like we're looking into an invisible world. And they seem to be following us everywhere on this island. Just like fetches."

"Like what?"

"They're these kinda ghost things. Dad told me about them. I think that's what we're seeing." I looked at her; she seemed dazed. "What do you think they are?"

"I don't know," Fiona answered slowly. "I just don't know what's real anymore."

Ranger Morrison was now a few feet away, staring at the dead goat. "I'm gonna radio the Mounties," he announced. The wind had picked up and was making the short, wide sleeves on his shirt flap.

"It's about time," Fiona whispered, low enough that he couldn't hear her.

Morrison walked to the edge of the slide, then stopped. "Oh my God," he said. He quickly made his way down the rope, disappearing from sight. A second later the boat started up.

"What's he doing?" Fiona asked. She stood and took a few steps toward the slide. "He's leaving us!"

I got to my feet, each bone creaking, and shuffled closer to the water, forcing myself to move. I pushed my cold hands deep into the pockets of my shorts.

Morrison was pulling away, yelling into his microphone. Far above him giant storm clouds gathered.

"Maybe he has to get out in the open to radio for help," I said.

Morrison put the microphone away. He circled over toward the cliff walls, where rocks pointed to the sky like teeth. The surf crashed against them. He stopped the boat as close to the jutting stone as he could, then plucked a long pole from the deck. It had a hook on one end.

I felt suddenly sick, staring out at the churning water and somehow knowing what I was about to see would be bad. Very bad. Is this what my sister experienced when she got one of those *good guesses*?

Then something else grabbed my attention. In the murky distance, out beyond the island, a form broke the surface. It was like a whale, but larger and too distant to discern. Waves washed up against it. I squinted. It slipped under the water.

A moment later it appeared again, farther away, then just as quickly disappeared. Had it been here feeding? Had we interrupted it?

I looked back down at Morrison. He'd just dipped the pole into the waves. He moved it around in a circular motion; then it caught on something heavy. With much effort he slowly hauled his catch into the boat.

It looked like a human body. With white, lifeless limbs.

It was about the size of Dad.

» 24 «

"Oh, no," Fiona whispered.

The boat revved up and Morrison turned it toward us. He cut through the water, slowing to a quick stop right next to the slide. He then bent over and urgently pushed down for a few moments. He was doing CPR. Finally he lifted the figure up.

I saw scraggly hair, a slightly balding forehead. Loose, swinging arms.

Dad, I thought. *Oh no. Not this … this can't happen to my father.*

He looked pale. He'd lost his glasses. What would I do if he was dead?

Then Morrison squeezed my father's stomach. Water sluiced out of Dad's mouth. He coughed for a few wretched moments, but didn't awaken. He was alive, at least.

My mind was a blur of questions, emotions. Had they tried to sacrifice him? Had he been thrown in the water and left to die? Would he survive this?

The ranger lowered him, gently resting his head on a pile of fishnets in the end of the boat. He yelled up to us, "Your dad was floating face down when I saw him. I thought he was dead, but he's still breathing. He's badly cut up though."

A wave slammed the boat against the slide. Morrison fell over, then cautiously pulled himself back to his feet, keeping a tight grip on the edge.

"Can we come down?" I hollered, gesturing to Fiona to get ready to climb down.

"In a moment. Somehow I'll have to get this boat steady."

The ocean was much rougher now. A thick, swirling breaker of clouds unfurled from the sky above us like a wave, lightning sparking its dark underbelly.

Within a minute it hit us full force. Ice-cold rain sliced down, biting into my skin. Wind struck my body. I stumbled back a few feet, struggled to keep my footing. Fiona and I leaned against each other. I grabbed her hand.

"We have to get down to the boat now!" she yelled. I nodded, shielding my eyes from the downpour. We had stumbled a yard or two away from the edge. I couldn't even see the water anymore. Or the boat.

But I thought I could hear the ranger yelling at us, his voice angry and urgent.

A clap of thunder shook the whole ravine, rattling my vertebrae. Lightning flashed directly above us, making the hair on the back of my neck shoot straight up. It was way too close for comfort.

Then a whispered song like a lullaby drifted into my ears.

Hullabulla lullabulla
bones and red blood
in a dark flood.

I turned to see where the song was coming from. Lightning shot down again, revealing a deep-blue, pencil-thin apparition standing in the ravine, one arm raised, like he was pulling strings on a puppet. A second later the figure was gone, swallowed by darkness.

"Fiona!" I screamed. "Let's go!"

I struggled to pull her right up to the edge of the slide. Her hand slipped out of mine, then immediately she shoved it back into my grip. She seemed to weigh a ton.

Then I heard her cry like she was a mile away from me, which didn't make any sense because I was still holding her hand. Her ice-cold fingers clung to mine.

I turned back to look at her. A specter scattered behind me, the feeling of someone's hand in mine disappeared. I heard ghostly laughter, then nothing. What was going on? A trick?

A fetch. It had to be. Doing its master's bidding.

Fiona yelled again. Her voice was muffled.

"Get down here!" Morrison shouted. He was struggling with the pole, prying at the rocks in an attempt to keep his boat from slamming against them. "This boat's gonna break apart any second!"

"Fiona's gone! Someone took her!"

"What? Get down here! Now! We'll bring the Mounties back and find her."

I took one look at the waves, him fighting against them. I saw the prone figure of my father laid out across the deck.

What was the sensible thing to do, I wondered. Climb down, get in the boat, retreat to the campground and wait for the police to unravel this mess? That was the sensible thing to do. But nothing about any of this was sensible. I couldn't do anything for Dad now. And I couldn't leave Fiona to these madmen.

"Come here!" Morrison commanded.

"No," I said, not sure if he could hear me. "No! Take my father back. I'll find Fiona."

The ranger yelled something at me as I started running wildly toward the end of the ravine.

25

The ground had grown slippery. Light had drained from the sky, soaked up by the clouds. Soon total darkness would fall. I scrambled around, hoping to discover a clue to where Fiona had gone.

In misty darkness I tripped over the body of the goat and fell, accidentally hugging its wet hide. Dank, dead air slipped out of its lungs. Its eyes were open and dull. I recoiled, falling back against the metal post.

So many sacrifices had happened right here. So much violence. And I was lying right in the center of it all. I felt paralyzed by claustrophobia. How many animals had died in this spot?

I wasn't going to be next. I pulled myself together, sat up. A glowing light caught my eye. I saw that the black obelisk at the edge of the ravine had been moved, revealing the mouth of a cave. The light had come from the inside.

I padded slowly up to the opening. It seemed to exhale an unearthly stench of carcasses and filth piled up and left to rot. I took my last deep gulp of air, pulled my collar up to cover my mouth, and crept inside. The interior was tall; glowing stalactites hung from the roof like the teeth of an enormous dragon. I took a few more steps, hesitant to go too far. I stopped, listened. My own breathing echoed in the corners.

I thought I could hear the sound of footsteps and voices somewhere deep in the rock.

Suddenly a shuffling noise came from just behind me.

I spun around in time to see a bulky figure step out from a hidden alcove. He filled the doorway, blocking the dim light.

I slowly backed away into the cave.

"Done be fraid," a thick voice slurred quietly. *"Im Sirska. Juz want talk."*

I stepped back, panicked, and hit a wall, bumping a stone. It rattled across the floor.

"Done be fraid." He shuffled a few feet in my direction, then stopped. He was a heavyset man, certainly not the one I'd seen pointing at us in the rain just moments ago. *"Im Sirska. Siroska. Frend."*

There was something familiar about what he was saying. I could almost make out the words. *Sirska. Siroska.*

And then it suddenly made sense. "You're Siroiska," I whispered. "Doctor Siroiska."

"Yessss," he rasped. His voice was so hoarse I could barely make out the words. *"Siroska, ma name. Once."*

"Then you're alive."

He slowly shook his head. A sad motion. *"No. Dead. Im dead. He killed me."*

"What?" I asked in disbelief.

"Bolverk. Sorcerer. He came to me in dreams. I was alone, doing my research. Hullabulla, he sang. He led me to his grave and I opened it. Then he killed me. On the rune stone."

"But, you're here, talking ..."

"Dead. Heart stopped beating many, many months ago. He kept

me like this to do his work. Never resting. So cold. Always another sheep. Another goat. Until everything was set."

Siroiska had gone crazy. That was the only thing that made sense. He'd spent a whole year trapped at this end of the island. And what was that about sheep and goats? He'd killed them?

"Dead," he repeated. *"All dead inside me. No more dreams."* He staggered into a shaft of dim light that came from some opening in the ceiling. I could make out his face now, checkered with gray and white patches, the skin hanging loose. His eyes were lifeless marbles that searched the room blindly for me. Was he out of his mind?

Or was he telling the truth?

He shook, struggled to take another step, then fell to his knees. *"He made me this way. He did this. I tried to warn you. To get you to go away."*

I remembered now. I'd seen Siroiska before, when we were running from the longhouse. He'd come out of the forest, waving his arms. "Who were you warning us about?"

"Bolverk. Evil spirit, now flesh." Bolverk, the name burned in my skull. Somehow I knew it had to be him. *"Bolverk chose you and your father, said he knows your bloodline, knows your family came from the same land as him. Many years ago. He tried to feed your father to the worm. It refused. Bolverk believes he will have better luck with a smaller gift."*

"Fiona? Is that what you mean? Where did he take her?"

Siroiska struggled to lift his finger. He pointed past me. *"There … there. Find her. If you can. She's there."* He was falling down farther, crumpling into himself. *"I'm fading. He no longer needs me. He has what he wants."* Siroiska was now collapsed in a heap on the floor. *"Leave me. I should have been gone long ago."*

"I'll send someone to get you. The Mounties are coming. You'll be safe again," I promised, knowing that somehow this was impossible.

He didn't answer.

I felt along the wall until I found an opening that went the same direction he'd pointed and started down the tunnel.

26

I traveled as quickly as I could, navigating over the rough ground. The walls around me glowed dimly.

I passed openings that led into other caves, all honey-combed beneath the earth. Some echoed with the sound of splashing waterfalls. Others smelled of decaying flesh. I tried to stick to the passage in the center, holding my arms out to stop from banging into a wall. I could only hope there weren't any hidden chasms.

Then I heard Fiona's voice. I turned a corner and pressed myself flush against the wall.

A dimly lit figure stood in the center of a chamber, one hand clasped on Fiona's arm. He was clad in dirty rags that hung in strips wrapped loosely around his body. He was tall, thin, his shoulders disproportionately wide. His face was hidden by a hood and he held a long, intricately carved staff in his hand. Circling around him were the two wolves; their claws clicked against the stone. Light emanated from somewhere. I looked for candles. Even a flashlight. Then it became apparent: the man himself was glowing softly.

"Let go of me!" Fiona moaned. "Please, let go!"

"Do you know me?" the raspy voice drifted out from somewhere inside his hood. Waves of dread filled the tunnel,

filled me. *"Do they still try to protect the children from me, the crib breaker? Do they still whisper the lullabies of fear?"*

Lullaballa bulla
the blood runs down
Lullaballa bulla
Bolverk wears darkness on his crown.

His singing was surprisingly soft and musical. It had a powerful effect, drawing me toward him. The bite on my arm flared with pain, began to burn, then turned cold. At some level I responded, moving forward, pulled by an irresistible force. First one step, then another. I was powerless to stop myself.

One of the wolves looked toward me, two red slits for eyes. I shuffled ahead, turning the corner. Then the echoes of his song died and I was able to hold myself still. The wolf slowly turned away. I edged back into my hiding place.

"Do they still sing of me?" Bolverk asked, a harsher edge to his voice. Fiona didn't answer. *"Do they fear my return?"*

"I —" Fiona sounded hoarse. He was squeezing her arm, forcing her to speak. "I — I don't know."

He met this with a long silence.

"So many years," he whispered, finally, *"the wolf chasing the sun. So many days spent sleeping, all the languages of men drifting into my skull. All the ancient dreams waiting for life. And then, to waken in my cairn wearing this filthy flesh. I will wear new flesh soon."*

He looked down at Fiona. *"You are small. Warm. The perfect morsel for a god."*

I remembered the goat that had been torn in half. I shuddered at the thought of the same thing happening to her.

"Tonight you shall rest in Niflheim. When you tell

Modgud your name and lineage, let her know it was Bolverk who sent you. And that I will never dwell in her halls."

Niflheim. The land of the dead. Fiona was doomed.

My arm was burning again. I looked down at it, squeezing with my other hand, trying to stifle the pain. The snake bite had begun swelling up and oozing dark blood. It was as if just being near Bolverk had caused the reaction.

Bolverk's voice faded—they were gone. I stepped into the chamber where they'd been, only to discover several openings, each wide enough to travel down. Fiona and Bolverk were in one of the tunnels now, but which one? In a fit of panic I chose one, ran through it, blood pounding in my ears. Everything was closing in on me, stalactites scraping my head, until finally I came to a dead end. Bones were scattered around as if something had been trapped there long ago.

I ran back to where I thought I'd started and picked another tunnel, running madly down it. Finally, at the edge of exhaustion, I stopped and leaned against a wall. All this aimless wandering wasn't getting me anywhere. But what could I do? I'd starve to death down here if I couldn't find a way out. No one would know what had happened to me. I thought of my father lying unconscious in the boat. Had Morrison been able to get him safely back to the campground?

What would my dad do in this situation? My sister? I tried to stay calm. Maybe that was the best thing, to just slow down.

I closed my eyes. Pictured Fiona. I couldn't even imagine what must be going through her mind. For the first time in all the madness, the thought of my father's pain, of Fiona's plight, was too much. Tears welled up in my eyes.

What could I do for either of them? For myself?

My arm throbbed again. My vision shifted; suddenly I could see that other world again. Several fetches were gathered in front of me, pointing and laughing at my suffering.

I couldn't stand it. I bellowed, kicking out at them, my legs going right through their bodies. This only made them cackle harder. I chased them until my lungs felt like they would burst. The fetches vanished with a hissing noise. Bad luck. That's all they were. Bad luck on four legs. Another sign that I was doomed.

Something reflected from the floor a few feet in front of me. I walked ahead to where I'd seen the flash. I found the object: it was small, round and metallic.

It was the dollar coin. Whether on purpose or by accident, Fiona had dropped it. Maybe my luck was changing.

I pocketed the coin. At least I knew I was going the right way.

A slight breeze brushed my face, carrying the scent of fresher air. I was closer to freedom than I'd thought.

I staggered ahead. A hundred yards. Two hundred. The cave ended abruptly and I found myself on the edge of a cliff that dropped eighty feet to the churning ocean. Night had fallen while I was under the earth; a full moon peered between clouds, casting pale light. To one side of the cave was a narrow path leading up through some trees. I followed it. Branches rattled above me. The trees didn't look like any I'd ever seen. They were twisted in on themselves and grown together like each branch was trying to strangle another.

How far away were Fiona and Bolverk? And what would I do if I caught up with them?

The gale was colder now, like some forgotten winter

wind had been waiting to be unleashed from the sky. My skin had turned to gooseflesh. My right forearm had swelled up and become deadened. I could barely move my fingers.

CRACK!

The noise came from behind me. Bolverk was here! Or his wolves.

I was about to run when a familiar voice snapped, "I told you to eat garlic."

» 27 «

It was Harbard, limping toward me out of the trees. A blue glowing light surrounded him; my vision had switched to that other world.

"You don't listen very well, do you?" he said. His brow was furrowed. He was soaking wet and dirty, as if he'd been crouching out here for hours. He gripped a small axe in his hands. "If you'd eaten garlic there wouldn't be any swelling and you wouldn't be seeing what you see now. The second sight isn't meant for one so young." He ran his hands in front of my eyes and the glowing light vanished. He pushed something into my right hand. "Squeeze this."

I slowly opened my deadened fingers and saw a smooth, palm-sized stone. Runes were scratched across its middle. "What … what is it?"

"A piece of rune stone. Like the ones that protect my house. It is etched with *helgan,* the word that will ease all wounds. And take away second sight."

A sharp pain pierced my arm. I squeezed the rock and the ache ebbed away.

"It works!

"Of course. Why wouldn't it?"

I felt my wrist. The bleeding had stopped.

From somewhere far ahead of us in the woods came a low thudding sound. "Where is …"

"The afturganga: the one who walks after death," Harbard said, simply. "Bolverk has gone on to complete his task." Harbard's teeth glinted in the moonlight; he looked almost savage. "My father buried him and his companions. Under stone. I should have seen the signs, that he was awake again." He grabbed my shoulder and pushed me down the path. "You will help me. We must move now, there is little time. Your friend is alive, but not for long."

I followed Harbard. He led me past tree after twisted tree; nothing seemed to have grown straight on this side of the island. A mist seeped out of cracks in the ground as if the earth was trying to cover up what was about to happen. Or was it old, malevolent spirits, forcing their way to the surface to watch? To add their evil to the night?

I shivered. Harbard stopped briefly to give me his jacket, then gruffly commanded me to keep moving.

The way grew even steeper. I used my left hand to grab at roots and small bushes and pull myself higher. Harbard moved quickly and with ease, his limp was hardly noticeable. I wasn't going to let any old man outdistance me.

We climbed, not stopping for anything. The wind had picked up again, swirling the fog around us. Pellets of rain stung my skin. We journeyed higher, step after step into the thickening gloom.

Soon a booming noise filled my ears. Deep, echoing drums laden with doom.

"He's begun!" Harbard quickened his pace, flicking mud and water all over me.

We reached the top, a small plateau covered with stones and outcroppings of rock. We crawled to the far side and peered over the edge. Below us was the small bay Fiona and I had fled in the boat.

"This is where the Mórar landed, so many lifetimes ago," Harbard said. "They climbed up onto the island and died, their bodies wasted from being at sea so long. Washed by rain, shrouded by snow. Their evil sank into the very depths of Drang."

The light of the moon penetrated the clouds, outlining everything. Tendrils of swirling mist floated above the water. There was a long rectangular rock near the edge of the bay, surrounded by waves. Torches had been fastened to each corner and were burning brightly, the flames flickering back and forth in the wind. The booming grew louder.

"Where is the sound coming from?" I asked.

"The Mórar. Bolverk's companions are in the underworld, standing on the shore of corpses, pounding the summoning drums. They are close to returning to life. That is why we can hear them so clearly."

I was silent. I couldn't comprehend what he was saying.

"Jormungand comes," Harbard said. "From the deep, they call him." The drums beat faster, heavier. "Once, many ages ago, Jormungand was a friend of my mother's people; the guardian of the island. A son of Sisutl." Harbard pointed at the rectangular rock. "The shaman would stand on that stone and speak with him. But now Bolverk has twisted the guardian, turned him into something vile. He taught the great serpent to eat the flesh of animals, not the green plants of the mother. Jormungand has refused to feed on your father. Bolverk hopes to lure him here and offer him smaller human flesh."

A motion attracted my eye: gray robes flapping in the wind. Bolverk was crossing the bay, dragging Fiona toward the rock. At the very sight of him Harbard sucked in his breath. So did I.

Both Fiona's wrists were bound together by ropes. Bolverk yanked her ahead, wading easily through the water. He pushed her down on the stone, but she twisted out of his arms, landing with a splash. She was going to get away!

Fiona kicked desperately through the waves, but she couldn't use her arms. She sank below the surface. Bolverk waited, unconcerned. I opened my mouth to yell at him, to get him to save her. Harbard gripped my arm, silencing me. A few moments later Bolverk reached into the water and pulled her into the air. She gasped, gulping in air.

Before she could get her bearings, he roped Fiona to two posts, tying her tightly so her arms were stretched out and she was forced to stand. Bolverk backed away.

Fiona struggled but the bonds were too tight. The waves crashed up against the stone below her.

Harbard got to his knees. "I must go down there."

"I'll go, too."

"No. You'd be little help. I must do this; my father taught me how to deal with him. But up here ..." Harbard seemed to smile slightly, "... yes, up here you will give me a big hand."

He reached into a holster on his belt, pulled out a pistol with a thick barrel.

"A gun? Do you expect me to shoot someone?"

"No. Bullets would mean little to Bolverk. This is a flare gun." I should have guessed by the size of the barrel. "Only one flare remains. I will signal and you'll fire it above Bolverk's head."

He handed the gun to me. It felt heavy and old like a

swashbuckler's pistol. I searched for a safety.

"Careful," Harbard whispered, "it has a hair trigger."

Then he started looking for a way down. A second later he was gone.

I settled into place, holding the flare gun with my left hand. Despite the healing stone my right arm was still useless, so I was worried about my aim.

Bolverk stood on the beach, his arms spread wide. The wind blew his garments into long, flowing ribbons that trailed behind him. He banged his staff in time with the drums. Waves washed in, splashing him.

Lightning sliced jaggedly through the sky, hitting a stone about thirty feet from me and pulverizing it. The heat seared my skin, left me momentarily blinded. Acrid smoke filled my nostrils.

I blinked. My sight returned and I could see Bolverk in the same place, chanting. The drums grew louder, more hypnotic; a beat as ancient as the earth. I found myself wanting to hit the drums, to stand and let the rhythms move through me. The sounds spoke of a past that lay half-forgotten inside my heart, as if I had once believed in all the old gods and spirits; believed the world had been formed in burning ice and biting flame.

For a split second my vision slipped back into that other place. Four hulking, glimmering figures were at the edge of the beach, pounding on transparent drums. Fetches danced around them, darting in and out.

The stone in my hand pulsed and the vision ended. At the same moment a massive form broke through the water, then disappeared. I stared at the shifting waves, now growing even higher.

Hurry, I thought, urging Harbard on, hurry!

I glimpsed a movement on the beach. Harbard had made his way to the bottom and was creeping around huge stones. A light rain drizzled down.

Another flash of lightning created two shadows above him on one of the rocks. Four-legged shapes with huge jaws. The wolves!

Harbard moved into the open, unaware he was being followed.

I yelled, but the drums and the crashing of waves were too loud. The wolves loped along, closing in for the kill.

"Harbard!" I screamed again. The wind ripped the words from my mouth.

I pointed the gun at the wolves. My hand was shaking and slick with sweat. I used my right hand to steady my aim. Pulled the trigger.

Click.

I pulled again. *Click. Click.* It wouldn't fire. The flare gun had become too wet or maybe it was too old. I tried to see how to open it, but in the dark it was impossible. I held the gun out once more and pulled the trigger all the way back.

SSST-POOM. A red flare fell like a comet, making Harbard turn. The light revealed the wolves leaping through the air. Harbard threw up his arms. Then darkness.

I dropped the gun, pushed myself up and ran as quickly as I could across the slippery rocks, searching for a path that would lead down along the rock walls. I searched desperately, squinting my eyes in the dark, and finally I discovered the narrowest of trails. I shoved the healing stone in my pocket and moved as quickly as I could along the path. The occasional bolt of lightning lit my way.

I only looked down once and that was enough. I was at least forty feet up from the ground. If I fell I'd be nothing but a pile of broken bones, to be feasted on by crows and flies.

I worked my way over rocks, bumping my side against the cliff. I slipped and grabbed at an outcropping to save my skin. The path grew narrower still. I clung to the wall, but my wounded arm was nearly useless. The rocks were sharp and slick. It was taking too long. Somewhere below me I heard the growl of a wolf. Harbard would be torn to pieces by now.

I quickened my pace.

A few feet ahead I could see the path widen. But first I had to cross a section just inches wide. I took a step. Then another. The ledge crumpled underneath my feet.

I plummeted down, arms flailing, looking for something to grab. Lightning flashed, revealing twisted, snake-like roots. I latched onto one, stopping my fall.

A second bolt of lightning revealed a single tree that had somehow clung to the side of the cliff for years, defying the rock, the lack of soil, defying the wind and rain that had pounded on it. The tree had worked its roots into the cliff wall and somehow found nourishment.

I held onto it tightly with my left hand, wrapping myself in the roots. Warmth returned to my limbs. The wind wasn't as harsh here. I had the odd feeling that the tree was lending me its strength. And then I remembered the dream my sister had told me about, the one with the Yggdrasill tree.

I felt her presence near me. I closed my eyes and thought I could hear my ancestors—my Grandma Gunnora, Grettir, Great Grandfather—all urging me on, whispering that I had work to do, my family's work passed down from generation to generation. I started to lower myself using the tree roots as ropes. Finally I reached the ground and could look across the bay.

The drums had stopped. One of the torches was out, the other flickered madly in the gale. Bolverk was gone. All I could see was Fiona on the rock, struggling against her bonds.

A few steps later I was splashing through six inches of water. The ocean was making its way, wave by wave, into the bay.

Closer, I heard the snarl of wolves. I spotted the outcropping where I thought Harbard was and hurried toward it.

I rounded the rock and there was Harbard, still very much alive, but cornered by two wolves.

» 29 «

The gray wolf was limping. It looked like Harbard had injured it with the small axe he gripped in his hand. But the wolves had done their own share of damage. Harbard's right arm was hanging down, blood dripping from a wound that had been torn above his elbow. He had a crazed look on his face as if the gash had turned him into a berserker.

The limping wolf moved to one side of Harbard, the black one to the other. Their hides had been stripped here and there, were flapping loose, revealing white ribs. The gray wolf had no fur on its legs at all, only white bones, clicking and clacking with each movement. Harbard moved back and forth, facing one wolf, then the other, but he couldn't change position fast enough.

The black wolf leaped, its mouth wide. Harbard spun and sank the axe into its skull. It fell dead, seemed to clatter into pieces. I was already running to Harbard when the gray wolf plowed into his back. Its jaws clamped down on his shoulder. He screamed and tried to roll away but the wolf had him. I jumped the final yard and tackled it, my head smashing into its ribs. I grabbed the wolf's fur, tried to pull it off Harbard, but bits of flesh and bone came loose in my hands. The pieces of flesh were cold as ice.

My ploy succeeded too well. The beast turned on me, fangs bared. Its tongue was black and dry. It dived for my throat and I fell back, pushing at it. Trying to keep it away.

Steel flashed. Harbard's axe was buried in the wolf's skull. It staggered, let out a low moan, then the red light of its eyes faded. It collapsed on top of me. I shoved the thing off me and rolled away from the revolting stench of the carcass.

Harbard was lying on his back, bleeding from the shoulder. "A bad throw," he said, his voice grave. "I was aiming to chop his head right off. But I *was* using the wrong arm."

A loud, grinding noise came from the water, like one of the cliffs had shifted closer. An unearthly moaning shook me to the core.

Water had splashed in and now reached up to Harbard's chest. He looked half awake. I got up and dragged him to higher ground. His eyes were rolling around in their sockets and he was moving in and out of consciousness. Without warning, he grabbed me, saying, "Ragnarok comes. The earth will be consumed by venom and fire," then closed his eyes.

I left him, pulled the axe out of the wolf's skull. Its body had mostly dissolved and was being bumped toward shore by waves. I was surprised how calm I was, as if I was seeing the most natural sight in the world.

The moaning was louder now. A sound that seemed to signal the end of the world.

I heard a cry for help. I dashed toward Fiona.

» 30 «

The water grew deeper, making it harder and harder to run. Bolverk was somewhere out of sight. I charged toward the stone, waded to the front of it and Fiona finally saw me. "Michael," she said, her voice hoarse, "I've had a very bad day."

"Hold still. I'll cut you loose."

I chopped at the rope, but it was thick and made of tightly bound hair. And I was handicapped, having to use my left hand. "Hit it again!" Fiona shouted. I struck twice more and the binding snapped. Fiona slipped to one side, then steadied herself.

"Take the axe," I yelled.

That familiar blaze entered her eyes. She grabbed the axe from me and whacked the rope again and again. The blade refused to bite. I climbed onto the stone, trying to find a way to help. A blast of wind nearly knocked us into the water.

Then, just as Fiona began to make headway, she stopped in mid-swing. "It's here," she whispered.

I glanced up as a glistening, vast shape crashed down into the waves. Part of the stone suddenly gave way. I slipped. The only thing that stopped me from rolling into the water was my grip on Fiona.

I pulled myself back and we scrambled to our feet. "I dropped the axe!" Fiona struggled against the remaining rope. "Help me untie this!"

I reached toward the rope, yanking at the knots. They were too tight and wet. We struggled together, trying to loosen them. Finally, success, and we both pulled. Fiona's arm was freed.

A hard object whacked my shoulder and I froze. Something blurred past my eye, struck Fiona and she, too, stood stiff.

Bolverk had arrived, his staff crackling with blue energy.

"Infidel!" Bolverk whispered. *"Ragnarok is here! You cannot stop the unstoppable."*

I still couldn't move. The wind hit me full force, but my feet were glued to the stone.

Bolverk stood beside us. *"Ormr,"* he bellowed. Words as ancient as all my ancestors, words that described nightmares. *"Midgardsormer."*

A roaring sound from the darkness answered him. The water began to bubble.

"Ormr," he spoke again.

Lightning slashed the sky, its light revealing a dark green form, moving toward us like a giant wave. A long snout floated in the air, the head rising higher and higher. Serpentine eyes the size of shields glared down, two glowing pools of rage. This was a face even Thor would fear.

"Jormungand," Bolverk whispered, *"son of Loki, accept these gifts."*

He bowed and stepped back a few yards, leaving Fiona and me frozen there.

The serpent's eyes flickered at us. This was the god of the island. Once a guardian of men, now an eater of flesh. It hovered like it was about to strike.

Sarah's voice drifted into my head. *I dreamed you will use a stone to shake the root of all the worlds.* I didn't know if it was her or a memory of her, but the words were clear.

What could it mean? What stone?

The feeling that my twin sister was somewhere nearby calmed me, loosened my arms. The stone, I thought, the healing stone. I slowly pushed my right hand into my pocket and pulled out the stone.

Jormungand watched me, breath hissing between his fangs.

But what was I to do? Throw it? Would that drive him away? I thought of Thor, how he had slain the serpent with his hammer, then had fallen down dead from the venom. Pitting anger against anger. Steel against tooth and coil. Was that the way to victory? How do you fight something so enormous it could swallow the sky?

I lifted the stone above my head, showing it to the snake. He glared and hissed again.

Anger couldn't be at the root of the world. Something always rose up again, always came back. Even in the Norse myths, when all the battles were fought and most of the gods dead, a new world rose from the old. A world of light and warmth. Of life. Grandpa had told me all about it.

"Friend," I spoke, my voice cutting through the wind. "You were once our friend."

I lowered my arm.

Jormungand blinked. He dropped his head slightly.

"No!" Bolverk cried. The serpent looked his way.

Bolverk was silent now. He lifted his staff, waved it slowly back and forth. Jormungand mirrored the movement, his head drifting from side to side. Finally, Bolverk held the staff still.

"Midgardsormer," he whispered.

Jormungand snapped open his cavernous mouth, displaying two fangs, dripping venom.

He lunged at us.

» 32 «

The stone platform disintegrated beneath our feet. Fiona and I were thrown into the water, the weight of the beast knocking us further down. Panicking, I kicked up with all my strength until I broke the surface. I could hear Fiona floundering through the waves beside me.

Just as I found my footing a hand grabbed me from behind and forced me back under. I slipped to one side and struggled up again. Bolverk clamped onto my shoulder. I hammered at him and his hood fell away, revealing his raging face, all white and skull-like, one socket empty, the other holding a large, glowering eye. His mouth was uncannily big and thick-lipped.

I pushed at Bolverk, then punched my fist into his eye and broke free, making him drop his staff.

"Meddling infidel!" Bolverk latched onto me again, digging his thin fingers into my neck. He lifted his free arm.

Jormungand rose up behind him, silently. Higher and higher, water dripping from his scales.

Bolverk seemed to sense the serpent's presence; he lowered his arm, released me and faced Jormungand. He began backing slowly away.

Jormungand dived, his mouth gaping, and Bolverk

screamed. Then was suddenly silent.

A massive wave knocked me to one side. The last thing I heard was Fiona yelling, "Michael!" Then I was under the water again, kicking against the pull of an undertow. Deeper. Deeper. Down to the bottom.

But something bumped me, forcing me through the water with one big whoosh. Lifting me up above the waves, leaving me near the shore. Fiona found me and we swam back together. I led us to the end of the bay, splashing through shallow water, finally climbing onto the rocks.

An immense and majestic serpentine shape rose in the distance, glinting with silver moonlight. I could just make out its shining eyes and a snake's snout before it dived gracefully into the ocean and was gone.

Together, Fiona and I had the strength to help Harbard to the top of the cliffs. He was in much better shape than when I'd left him, though his arm seemed broken. "It's just a scratch," he said. He guided us to where he'd left his ferry.

He wouldn't let us drive. He planted his feet, grabbed the wheel tightly and piloted us through the water. The sun was just beginning to rise, bringing color back to the world.

When we reached Harbard's cabin, his dog greeted us at the door.

"You don't have to fear him," Harbard said. "Surt knows the difference between good and bad. Unlike many people."

The dog stepped aside and we went in. I was surprised to find Harbard had a TV and a police radio.

Soon we had the Mounties on the line and were told to wait right where we were. They informed me my father had been taken on a fisherman's boat to a hospital in Nanaimo before the storm had completely enveloped the island. He was in intensive care, but he had come to and asked about me.

Dad was going to be alright. It took a moment for this to sink in.

Harbard kept talking about axe ages and sword ages

and wind ages and wolf ages. He seemed lost in some strange world. At one point he looked me in the eyes and smiled. "Snake slayer," he said.

We had to wait for a long time. Fiona told me what it was like to be in the caves with Bolverk. We didn't talk about Jormungand or anything else after that. It seemed too soon. She eventually fell asleep, but I found that even a snooze was an impossible prospect. There was too much to think about. I couldn't slow my brain down. I kept hearing Bolverk's final scream and seeing the serpent disappear beneath the waters.

The bite on my arm had nearly disappeared, though it still ached.

Hours later several RCMP officers showed up, along with Ranger Morrison. "You're a brave kid," was all he said to me. Then a gray-haired Mountie named Sergeant Olson introduced himself. He and another officer asked me questions and I answered as best as I could, telling them what I thought they would believe. When they were finished, the sergeant shook my hand, which still hurt. He said a ride to the hospital was waiting for me in Port Hardy. Then he left to try and find any sign of Bolverk.

I found out later that the Mounties discovered the bones of a man in the caves. They used dental records to prove it was Siroiska. The coroner said he'd been dead for over a year. Days later a huge human skull with one extraordinarily large eye socket washed up on shore. It dissolved in a Mountie's hands.

About twenty minutes after the police left, Harbard got up and convinced us that only he could get us home across the water. "I won't even charge you," he said.

Soon we were in his ferry, cutting through the waves. I

sat beside Fiona at the back. I looked out nervously at the ocean.

"Jormungand sleeps now," Harbard whispered. He must have caught my glance. "We'll make it to the other side."

He was right. The water was calm and easy, the ferry cutting a smooth path through it. Harbard's prediction about my father and me had turned out to be right. Only one of us did return with him. I was just thankful it hadn't been any worse for Dad.

We landed at a small dock on an island. Cabins were set on a hill, looking down on us. It seemed too real, too perfect, after being on Drang. Fiona got off and I climbed onto the pier with her.

"Well, I guess this is it," she said. "Goodbye, so long and all that. I hope you'll drop me a note sometime, let me know whether you've made it home."

"You know, I learned something these past few days," I said.

"What?"

"That if I can make friends with you, I can probably make friends with anyone."

She grinned, showing her dimples.

Then I did something that completely surprised me. I kissed her. Quickly. On the lips. I stepped back.

Fiona stood there, stunned. For the first time since I'd met her, she was speechless.

"Goodbye," I said. "You'll have to try a holiday in Missouri sometime. It's nowhere near as weird."

She nodded but didn't answer.

I got back in the ferry and Harbard started to slowly pull away. Fiona was still staring at me. Finally she pointed and her shout drifted across the water. "I'll write you!" she promised, "as long as you don't tell me any more Norse stories!"

I must have smiled for the rest of the trip. Before I knew it we'd landed at Port Hardy and I stepped onto the dock with a great sigh of relief.

Harbard grinned. For him there were no long farewells. "Good-bye, Thor," he said. Then he was heading away, as if it had been just another day's work.

A tall, middle-aged Mountie was waiting at the end of the pier. He led me to his car and we headed to the hospital to see my father.

Dad would finally have the perfect chapter to end his book.